Justice Rules

Janet Sierzant

Justice Rules
Copyright © 2025 Janet Sierzant
ISBN: 978-1-970153-46-0
Library of Congress Control Number: 2024904945
Distribution: Ingram Book Company

Special acknowledgment to beta readers Debbie Santoriello, Donna Qualia, Ellen Contreras, and George Ireland.

Maison
La Maison Publishing
Vero Beach, Florida
The Hibiscus City
lamaisonpublishing@gmail.com

Heist

Carl leaned against the car, cigarette dangling from his lips, his tie knotted too tightly for the heat.

He flicked the butt into the gutter. "Get in, Justine — and make it quick."

"Geez, what's your hurry?" she muttered, grimacing as she slid into the front seat. The overpowering scent of cologne made her gag. "What's with the tie? You hate ties."

"Can't a guy look respectable?"

"Respectable isn't your style. What's going on?"

He patted her hand. "Don't you worry your pretty little head, darlin'."

"After today, our money problems will be a thing of the past."

The words should have comforted her, but they landed like a stone in her gut. "Why? Where are we going?"

Justine forced a smile. She'd heard that tone before, half charm, half demand, and it always meant trouble.

The afternoon sun hung high over the town square, gilding the clock tower in a bath of golden light. When the bell chimed, she shivered. Something in her bones told Justine Morgan she'd never hear it again. Her pulse quickened.

Carl pulled over near the corner, where a stranger stood looking around like he was casing the place.

Justine's stomach tightened. "Who's that?" she whispered. "What are you doing?"

"I'll be back in a flash. Slide over and keep the engine running."

Before she could protest, Carl jumped out and slammed the door.

Justine slid into the driver's seat. She'd never been able to say no to Carl, even from the start—but this time, a cold dread settled in her gut. She tapped her foot against the gas pedal, revving the engine.

Minutes dragged like hours. Then Carl came running back, the front of his shirt bloody and torn. He yanked the door open, eyes wild.

"Drive!"

Her gaze dropped to the pistol in his hand. "Where did you get that gun?"

"Stop asking questions!" he shouted, shoving it into the glove compartment.

The wail of sirens pierced the air. Justine froze, hands trembling on the wheel.

"Step on it!" Carl barked.

She slammed the car into gear, its tires squealing as it shot down the narrow road. The smell of blood made her feel sick. "What did you do?" she cried, tears blurring the road ahead.

"Faster!"

Something thudded beneath the tires. Justine gasped. "Oh my God, Carl — did I just hit someone?"

"It was a dog. Don't look back."

"A dog?" Her stomach heaved. She veered off the road, the car lurching into a ditch. Mud sucked at the tires as she tried to reverse.

"Damn it, Justine! You're so stupid." He grabbed the gun again and leapt out of the car, fury etched across his face.

"Hit the gas gently, I'll push."

Her mind was jelly. On the fourth try, the car lurched free.

Carl pulled open the driver's door, shoving her aside. "Move!" He floored it toward the highway, but red and blue lights blazing, cut them off — two patrol cars ahead, two behind.

Carl cursed and slammed on the brakes. He bolted into the woods as gunfire cracked through the air.

Justine sat frozen, staring at the approaching officer.

"License and registration," he said coldly. His voice was almost surreal.

She fumbled in her purse for her license and rifled through the glove compartment.

"Step out of the vehicle. You're under arrest."

"Please... you don't understand," she whispered.

But the officer showed no sympathy. He cuffed her wrists and placed her in the back of the squad car.

At the station, she was booked and processed. The officer instructed her to face forward, then turn to the right and left. She kept her expression blank, staring at the wall instead of the camera. After her mugshot, she was fingerprinted and taken to a holding cell.

*****

Before her arraignment, Justine sat across from her court-appointed attorney, Mr. Henderson.

"Don't worry," he said. "They rarely give serious time to accomplices. Your boyfriend will take the brunt of it. All you have to do is plead guilty."

"But I'm innocent!"

"I'm sure you are. But going to trial is risky."

"I won't plead guilty. I won't."

"Do you want to risk fifteen years in prison?"

"No... I—"

"Then listen to me. Throw yourself on the court's mercy."

Justine nodded reluctantly.

He gathered his papers and snapped his briefcase shut. "Do you need a ride to the courthouse?"

"No. I'm with my father."

"Okay. I'll meet you there."

Justine and her father drove to the federal courthouse in Orlando. Inside, she noted the worn wood paneling rich with history. The scent of cypress resins, old varnish, and citrus wax once reminded her why she'd wanted to study law. Now, it just smelled musty.

When she entered the courtroom, she saw her attorney, Ronald Henderson. He wore a baggy blue suit and scuffed pointed-toed shoes that looked like they came from a thrift store. He was in his fifties, with a beak-like nose and a grin that didn't belong in a courtroom.

The Florida State Prosecutor, Agatha Holt, sat at the next table. In her late thirties, fit and poised in a gray skirt suit and heels, she radiated confidence. Her dark eyes bore into Justine, making her knees tremble.

She took a seat beside her lawyer and waited.

"The Nineteenth Judicial Circuit Court of St. Lucie County is now in session," the bailiff announced. "The Honorable Patrick McKinney presiding."

Everyone stood.

Judge McKinney, a pale man in his sixties with tired eyes and a doughy complexion, entered the courtroom, his robes swishing like a heavy curtain. His pale face betrayed no emotion as he settled into his high-backed chair.

After reviewing the file, he glanced around the room. "Please be seated," he said, adjusting his glasses. "Let the record reflect all are present."

Justine lowered herself into her chair.

Her father sat stiff in the front row, his jaw clenched, his eyes fixed on the floor.

She wanted to draw strength from him, but he looked as though he'd already given up.

"How does the defendant plead?"

"Not guilty, Your Honor," Henderson said.

Trial

On the morning of the trial, Justine slipped into the navy-blue skirt set—one of two outfits her mother had bought her at Macy's. Skipping makeup, she pulled her long brown hair into a ponytail and went downstairs.

"You look nice," Kathleen said, straightening the collar of Justine's blouse. "Blue is your color."

"Thank you for taking me shopping, Mom. I needed something conservative to wear to court. Most of my formal clothes were donated when I moved in with Carl. The closet was too small."

"I still don't understand why you moved in with him."

"I wish I'd listened to you. I thought I was in love. Things were great at first, but Carl changed. I couldn't see a way out. He really scared me."

"All you had to do was tell us, dear. You know your father would've stepped in to protect you."

"I didn't want to admit anything was wrong. I convinced myself I could change him."

"Men like that don't change — they only get worse. You're lucky he didn't hurt you."

"He slapped me once and said it was my fault for provoking him."

"That should've been your signal to leave. All of this could have been avoided."

"I'm sorry I disappointed you."

Kathleen's expression softened. "You're free of him now. That's what matters."

"I'm not free yet, Mom. I still have to face the court."

Her mother reached into her apron pocket. "I have something for you."

"What is it?" Justine asked.

"It's the cross I gave you for your First Holy Communion." She opened her hand to reveal the small silver pendant. The tiny diamond in the center sparkled. "I'd feel better if you wore this in court today," she said. "God won't let anything bad happen to you."

Justine had been raised Catholic, attending Mass every Sunday, but after her confirmation, she'd begun to question her faith and stopped going to church.

Still, she let her mother fasten the chain around her neck and ran a finger over the cross. Despite her mother's faith, the possibility of prison loomed like a guillotine above her head.

Benjamin entered the kitchen. "Are you ready?"

"Yes, Dad."

Kathleen hugged her tightly. "I'm sorry I can't come with you today. The doctor says my heart is still unstable, even after the bypass."

"That's okay, I understand. The last thing I need, Mom, is for you to have another heart attack. I couldn't bear the thought of losing you."

Benjamin didn't speak for the entire drive. Traffic was heavy and made the trip feel longer. Finally, they arrived, and he parked in the lot outside the courthouse.

Justine took her seat next to her attorney and poured water into one of the two glasses on the table.

Judge McKinney made his entrance, and everyone stood up.

"Be seated," he said, reviewing his notes. He turned to the jury of nine women and three men. "Good morning. I trust you will use prudence to arrive at a just verdict based on the evidence."

He polished his glasses with the hem of his robe, then turned to the prosecutor. "You may call your first witness, Ms. Holt."

The prosecutor rose with the confidence of someone who had already won. Her heels clicked against the polished floor like a metronome as she approached the podium. "The State calls Rita Dillon."

A white-haired woman stepped forward, her handbag clutched in front of her like a shield.

She was sworn in and took her seat at the witness stand.

"Mrs. Dillon," Holt began smoothly. "How do you know the defendant?"

"She's my tenant's girlfriend," Rita said, her voice quavering but firm.

"Did you know Justine was living with Carl Davis?"

Rita hesitated. "No, well, yes. At first, Carl said she was just visiting. But I knew he was lying."

"And yet, you allowed them to stay?"

"He paid rent on time. I didn't see the harm. But if I'd known they were criminals...."

"Objection!" Henderson roared, finally stirring beside Justine. "Speculation."

"Sustained. The jury will disregard the last statement," the judge said.

Holt gave a satisfied nod. "No further questions."

The judge turned to Henderson. "Cross-examination?"

Henderson waved a hand. "Not at this time, Your Honor."

Justine's stomach dropped. *Not at this time?* He hadn't asked a single question.

"Mrs. Dillon, you may step down," the judge said.

As Rita left the stand, Henderson leaned toward Justine. "Do you know anyone else who can help your case?"

"Yes," she whispered. "Me. I want to testify."

His eyes widened. "You can't! You don't have to. The Constitution protects you from...."

"I have to," she insisted. "I'm the only one who knows the truth."

He sighed. "Your Honor, the defense calls Justine Morgan."

Judge McKinney raised an eyebrow. "Does your client understand she is not required to testify?"

"Yes, Your Honor."

"Very well. Call your witness."

Justine's legs felt like lead as she walked to the stand. She placed her hand on the Bible, swore the oath, and sat down. The wooden chair was cold against her back.

"Ms. Morgan," Henderson began, his voice oddly flat, "did you have any prior knowledge of this crime?"

"No," she said quickly. "I didn't know Carl was going to rob the jewelry store. I swear."

A voice exploded from the gallery. "You're a liar. You drove the getaway car!"

Gasps rippled through the courtroom. Another woman jumped up. "You killed my dog! You ran it down like it was nothing!"

The words struck Justine like a slap.

"I didn't mean to," she sobbed. "It was an accident!"

"She's a murderer!" the woman screamed. "She ran over my puppy!"

The judge's gavel cracked like thunder. "Order! Bailiff, remove that woman!"

The gallery erupted in murmurs as the bailiff dragged the woman out.

Justine clutched the tissue the judge handed her, but her hands shook so badly that she could barely hold it.

The jurors shifted in their seats, some looking away, others narrowing their eyes.

"Objection," Henderson said weakly. "Move to strike."

"Sustained," the judge replied. "The jury will disregard."

Justine knew they wouldn't.

"Any further questions, Mr. Henderson?"

"No, Your Honor."

"Ms. Holt, cross-examination?"

The prosecutor rose, her gaze sharply focused on Justine as she approached the stand. "You're still under oath, Ms. Morgan."

"Yes, ma'am."

"Do you go to church?"

"I—I was raised Catholic."

"Objection," Henderson said. "Irrelevant."

"Overruled," the judge said. "Keep it limited, Ms. Holt."

"Do you currently practice your faith?" Holt pressed.

Justine touched the cross at her neck. "No, ma'am."

"Were your suitcases in the trunk that day?"

"Yes, but Carl told me to pack—"

"Just yes or no?"

"Yes."

"You were behind the wheel on March 28th, correct?"

"I didn't have a choice. Carl—"

"Yes or no?"

"Yes, but—"

"Do you always do what people ask of you, Ms. Morgan?"

"No, I..."

"You didn't stop when you heard the sirens, did you?"

"I was confused. Carl was yelling. He had a gun."

"So you were in control of the vehicle."

"No—yes, but—"

"No further questions," Ms. Holt said, her voice crisp with finality.

"No!" Justine cried, but the gavel silenced her.

"Step down, Ms. Morgan," the judge ordered.

Her legs wobbled as she returned to her seat, the weight of the jury's stares pressing down on her.

"Any other witnesses?" the judge asked.

"No, Your Honor," Ms. Holt replied. "The prosecution rests."

"The defense?"

"No, Your Honor," Henderson mumbled.

Judge McKinney checked his watch. "This court is adjourned until tomorrow," he said and slammed his gavel.

Jury

Under the shower's powerful spray, Justine let the hot water scald her skin and tried to wash away the weight of the trial. She wondered if she'd made a mistake by rejecting the plea deal. Her attorney wanted to call Carl to the stand, but she dreaded seeing him again. Maybe his testimony would help her—maybe it wouldn't. Either way, she couldn't imagine facing Carl's eyes again—the same eyes that once charmed her now terrified her.

Switching the water to cold shocked her back to herself. Shivering, she stepped out, toweled off, and slipped into her undergarments. After debating whether to wear pants or a skirt, she chose the skirt and a simple white blouse.

Downstairs, her father sat at the table reading the morning paper, while her mother buzzed around the kitchen.

"Good morning, dear," Kathleen said. "I made you breakfast."

"I'm not really hungry, Mom."

"Please, you have to eat something. Just have the eggs—they're good protein. You'll need your strength."

"I don't think I can keep anything down."

"At least have a piece of toast, sweetheart."

"All right," Justine said, nibbling on the bread just to appease her.

Benjamin folded the paper. "It's time," he said quietly.

Justine's mother insisted on coming to court that day. She sat beside her husband, her eyes already glassy with tears.

A restless crowd had gathered outside the courthouse, clearly fueled by a media frenzy. Cardboard signs bobbed over their heads, in the humid air, ink running from last night's rain.

'THROW THE BOOK AT HER!' Their eyes were filled with open resentment.

Justine, escorted by an armed guard, hurried through a side door.

Inside, reporters rushed the hallways, shouting and scribbling notes. A line of police officers flanked the courtroom entrance like sentinels.

When Judge McKinney entered the room, everyone rose to their feet.

"Good morning," he said to the jury. "Today, we will hear from the defense." He shuffled through his paperwork. "Let's proceed. Mr. Henderson, you may call your first witness."

Henderson stood. "The defense calls Dr. Theodore Russell from the University of Miami."

Justine suspected her father had reached out to the professor on her behalf.

Dr. Russell, tall and composed, walked to the witness stand and was sworn in.

"Dr. Russell, how do you know the defendant?" Henderson asked.

"She was a student of mine."

"What course did you teach?"

"Ethics. It was a prerequisite for law students. Justine was studying to become a lawyer. She was highly motivated — at the top of her class."

"Have you had contact with her since?"

"No. I haven't seen Ms. Morgan since that class. But she struck me as a stand-up individual. I believe she's been wrongly accused."

"No further questions, Your Honor," Henderson mumbled.

The judge turned to the prosecution. "Cross-examination, Ms. Holt?"

"No, Your Honor."

"You may step down, Dr. Russell."

Henderson glanced at his notes. "The defense calls—"

But before he could continue, Ms. Holt stood. "Your Honor, the prosecution calls Officer Shanie."

The arresting officer — an arrogant man intoxicated by authority — strode to the stand, placed his hand on the Bible, and was sworn in. His dark eyes pinned Justine before the prosecutor spoke.

"Good morning, Officer Shanie," Ms. Holt began.

"Good morning."

"Thank you for your service."

"No thanks are needed, ma'am. I love what I do."

"Do you recall the afternoon of March 28th?"

"Yes. My partner and I got a radio call about a jewelry store robbery. We were told to look for a blue Camaro headed west toward I-95."

"And did you pursue the vehicle?"

"Yes. It was located on a dirt road near Highway 70. One of the suspects fled into the woods. My partner gave chase, and I secured the second suspect."

"Did she say anything when you arrested her?"

"She begged me to let her go. She tried to bribe me."

"That's not true!" Justine cried out.

Judge McKinney slammed his gavel. "Control your client, Mr. Henderson."

"No further questions at this time, Your Honor," said Ms. Holt.

Justine scribbled frantically on the notepad. *Do something, Mr. Henderson.*

Clearing his throat, Henderson rose. "Your Honor, I'd like to cross-examine."

"Very well," the judge said, rubbing his temple. "But don't badger the witness."

Henderson approached the stand. "Officer Shanie, was Justine driving the getaway car?"

"No. The driver ran. Ms. Morgan was in the passenger seat."

"So she didn't flee. She didn't resist arrest."

"She tried to persuade me to let her go."

"How is that resisting arrest?"

"Are you calling me a liar?"

"No, not at all."

"I've been an officer in good standing for over twenty-five years. I find your question offensive."

"No further questions, Your Honor," Henderson mumbled, retreating to the defense table.

"Thank you, Officer Shanie," the judge said. "You may step down."

Rubbing his eyes, Judge McKinney addressed the jury. He explained the charges and gave instructions on how to deliberate based on the evidence. Then he released them to begin deliberations.

"This court is adjourned," he announced.

As the jury filed out, Justine tried to read their faces — but none of them looked her way.

She felt sick. Holt had painted her as cold and complicit. Henderson's defense had landed with all the force of a wet sponge — limp and soggy.

Guilty as Charged

Justine's fate lay in the hands of twelve strangers.

It only took two hours for the jury to come to a decision — a bad sign for Justine.

When the court reconvened, the grim-faced jurors filed into the room. Justine tried to read their expressions. Some wore faint smiles; others looked solemn. Her pulse thundered in her ears.

"Has the jury reached a verdict?" Judge McKinney asked.

"We have, Your Honor," the foreman replied.

The bailiff approached the bench and handed the judge a folded slip of paper. Tension filled the air. Justine's heart pounded; she was certain everyone could hear it.

The foreman read aloud: "We, the jury, find Justine Morgan guilty of conspiracy to commit armed robbery."

Justine's hope was extinguished — snuffed out like a candle in a storm.

With contempt in his eyes, Judge McKinney turned to her. "Justine Morgan, please rise."

Justine tried to rise out of the chair, but her legs felt wobbly.

"In the case of the State of Florida vs. you have been found guilty."

The courtroom fell into a stunned silence.

"Damn it," her lawyer muttered. "You should've taken the plea deal."

The judge continued, voice heavy with judgment. "This is a tragedy for everyone involved. A man lost his life and deserves justice. Though you were not directly responsible for his death, you played a role in the crime."

He paused and glanced toward Justine's father.

"Given that this is your first offense, I will not impose the maximum sentence. Instead, I hereby sentence you to five years at the Larsen Correctional Institution."

Benjamin had always believed in the law, but now his daughter was being sent to prison. Beside him, Justine's mother sobbed into his shoulder.

"Five years?" Justine repeated in disbelief.

Her knees buckled, and she fainted forward.

When she came to, her lawyer hovered over her. "I'm sorry," he said quietly. "I told you—the plea bargain was the safer path. You knew the risks."

Instead of heading for law school, the law was sending her to prison. No one thought it would come to this. But Florida's new laws held accomplices nearly as accountable as the perpetrators.

As she was led away in handcuffs, Justine turned for one last look. Her mother wept into a handkerchief. Justine wanted to run back and comfort her, but the guards hustled her out the side door toward a waiting van.

The driver—a young man with a blank expression—barely noticed her tears. No one helped her out of the van when it arrived at the jail. She lost her balance as she stepped down and landed face-first onto the pavement. A guard grabbed her by the arm and hauled her to her feet.

Inside, a female officer pushed her against a wall to pat her down, then led her to a holding cell.

"Someone will be here shortly to escort you to the prison," the officer said before walking away.

"Can I use the bathroom before you go?"

"The bathroom's down the hall. I'll need permission to let you out."

Justine waited. The officer never returned.

Three hours later, two corrections officers—a man and a woman—entered the holding area. The female guard cuffed her wrists.

"Please," Justine said. "I really need to use the bathroom."

The two exchanged a look.

"Let the poor girl go," the male guard said. "It's a long ride to Larsen Penitentiary."

"All right," the woman said, "but the cuffs stay on."

They led her to a tiny restroom. Justine was grateful she'd worn a skirt, though she struggled to lower her underwear. Thankfully, her wrists were cuffed in front.

Next, they took her to the underground garage, where another van waited. The driver leaned against the vehicle, smoking a cigarette. Despite the open window, the smoke clung to the air inside.

His partner climbed in with the transportation paperwork, and the engine rumbled to life.

Justine sat in the back, alone, listening to the dispatch radio crackle. The officers were instructed to pick up other prisoners along the way.

By the time they left town, four other women had joined her in the van. One, a girl in her early twenties with thick black eyeliner, stared out the window, tears streaking her mascara.

Justine looked out at the people walking to school and work, entirely unaware that their lives could change in a blink.

She would have given anything for another chance — for sunlight on her face, for freedom.

Instead, she was on her way to prison for five years.

She'll be young enough to start a life afterward — to get married, have children. But she wasn't sure she'd ever trust another man again.

Prison

Larsen Correctional Institution sat forty-five minutes away, but for Justine, it might as well have been another world. On the prison bus, there were only two kinds of women — new arrivals like Justine, tense and wide-eyed, and repeat offenders, hardened by time. The veterans wore their bravado like armor, their fists ready to settle any dispute. Justine sat quietly among them, doing her best to appear calm while anxiety churned in her stomach.

The prison bus baked under the hot Florida sun as it waited for the large steel gates to open. Once through the guard station, the vehicle rolled slowly into the yard, surrounded by towering chain-link fences topped with coils of razor wire.

She stared out the window, her reflection ghosted against the glass. Her thoughts raced. All her life, she had wanted to be a lawyer. Now, she was on the wrong side of the law, her dreams evaporating with every turn of the wheels.

The bus came to an abrupt halt, jarring her back into the moment. One by one, the inmates jumped down. Justine followed, her eyes scanning the courtyard nervously. Groups of women watched the new arrivals with predatory interest, as if sizing up merchandise. Some smirked, others whispered, but most just stared, their faces unreadable.

They were led to the admission building. Justine's picture was snapped and affixed to an ID card labeled with her Department of Corrections number — 60456. That number, not her name, would be her identity from now on. She was handed a plastic cup and directed to a bathroom to provide a urine sample for drug screening.

"Can I call my mother?" she asked the female officer when she returned with the cup. "She has a heart condition. I don't want her to worry."

"You can purchase a phone card," the officer replied curtly, "but not until you're settled in."

Justine nodded, defeated. Until that moment, everything had felt like a bad dream. Now, reality was starting to sink in.

She followed the others down a dim hallway until they reached the processing area. One by one, each woman entered a room in her street clothes and emerged in prison garb. When it was Justine's turn, she stepped inside and came face to face with a large redheaded guard whose name tag read *Doris*. Her thick arms folded across her chest, and she barked her orders in a sharp German accent.

"Take off your clothes. Everything. Put them in this bag."

Justine hesitated but complied, stripping slowly under the woman's gaze. She dropped each item into the bag: shoes, pants, shirt, bra,... until only her panties remained.

"Panties, too!" the guard snapped impatiently, irritated with Justine's hesitation.

Slipping out of her underpants, Justine stood naked in front of the strange woman, who seemed to take pleasure in her humiliation.

"Now, turn around, bend over, and spread your cheeks."

Justine complied, but her stomach knotted with the snap of a rubber glove. The degrading search left her trembling as the guard's gloved finger violated her dignity.

"Cough!"

"Cough?"

"You heard me. Cough."

Justine cleared her throat and let out a small huff, trying to keep her balance on wobbly legs.

"Again. This time, like you mean it."

Feeling like she would pass out if she stayed in the position a moment longer, Justine took a deep breath and coughed.

"Okay, get up and turn around."

Her legs shook as Justine rose to face the guard.

"Remove your scrunchie, too."

"Why? Do you think I'm going to hang myself with it?"

The officer yanked it from her head, and Justine's hair fell over her shoulders. The smirked and guard looked down at her legs.

"What's that on your ankle?"

"It's a tattoo."

The correctional officer looked a little closer and let out a harsh laugh. "The scales of justice. Isn't that poetic?"

"I was in law school when I got it," Justine said to soften the guard.

"Well, young lady, looks like the scales aren't in your favor." Doris handed her a pile of ill-fitting prison clothes and a pair of orange slip-on sandals. "You can wear these until you're issued boots. Here's a blanket, a towel, and your pillow."

"May I have some soap? A toothbrush?"

The guard let out a dry laugh. "What do you think this is, the Ritz? You'll get a bar of soap and a toothbrush at orientation. Anything else, you buy from the commissary."

"I don't have any money," Justine said quietly.

"Then I suggest you make some friends fast — or call someone on the outside who gives a damn." Doris turned to the officer outside the door. "Take her to her cell."

Justine was led along the corridor of the maximum-security wing, averting her eyes from a few inmates who yelled obscenities. They behaved like construction workers. Amid the catcalls and whistles, some spat through the bars, and one even threw a used tampon. Before she could duck, it struck her forehead with a sickening thud.

The male guard dug through his pocket and pulled out a tissue. Justine wiped at the foul mess, but the foul odor clung to her skin.

The noise subsided, and they walked — the screams and taunts replaced by the hum of the fluorescent lights. They entered a long tunnel. Justine looked up at the small windows on the ceiling, each covered by bars, allowing slivers of sunshine to stream in. At the far end, another steel door led to the East building, where the minimum-security prisoners were housed. The guard sorted through the keys until he found the one he needed. Inside, the atmosphere was quieter, but not exactly welcoming.

Justine was checked in and assigned cube number thirty-four in a dorm-style unit, watched over by a central glass-enclosed guard station. The cubicles were separated by concrete dividers, each with two bunk beds.

"Hi. I'm Penny," said a bubbly young woman in her thirties, her mousy brown hair piled into a messy bun. She pointed to the older woman reading on the lower bunk. "That's Stella. She's been here twenty years and still has four and a half to go."

Justine offered a quiet "Hi," but Stella didn't look up.

"Camila has the bunk under yours," Penny continued. "She called dibs on the bottom after Tina left. Sorry, you're on top."

Justine glanced at the bare upper bunk. "Where is Camila now?"

"At the visitor center with her boyfriend. He's a total loser, but she's in love."

"What's she in for?"

"Two pills. Felony trafficking. 4-year mandatory — can you believe that?"

A loud buzzer cut Penny off. Women filed out of their cubes and lined up. "Prisoner count," Penny whispered.

Just then, a striking Latina with glossy black hair slid between them. Her top buttons were undone, and her full lips curled into a flirtatious smile.

"Hi. I'm Camila," she said softly to Justine.

The guard patrolling the line paused, giving Justine a long, appraising look. "We have new blood, ladies." She turned to Camila. "Button your shirt."

Camila grinned as she complied, clearly used to the attention.

After the headcount, the women marched to the cafeteria. The smell of greasy beef and gravy made Justine nauseous. She gagged, fighting to keep down the toast she forced herself to eat that morning.

"The first day is the hardest," Penny said, trying to offer comfort.

Justine managed a nod but didn't speak.

After dinner, Penny and Camila strolled to the media center to watch television. Justine didn't feel very social, so she went to her cubicle. All she could think about was ending the day.

She tried to get comfortable on the thin rubber mattress, which made her body sweat. The sound of a woman crying kept her awake.

When she couldn't sleep as a child, her mom used to tell her, "Think of something pleasant." She closed her eyes and tried to summon her mother's face. A train whistle echoed in the distance, and finally, she drifted off. She was awakened by a flashlight beam shining on her face. Her eyes popped open, and her pulse spiked. The guard's flashlight beam lingered, then moved to the next bunk. Penny and Stella didn't stir, and Camila rolled her head toward the cinderblock wall.

That night, lying awake in her bunk, she couldn't stop her mind from drifting backward, to a time when everything still felt possible. She had been in her senior year at the University of Miami, preparing for law school, when she met Carl Davis in a criminal justice class. He was older, streetwise, with a quick wit and a glint in his eye. She laughed at his jokes—even the crude ones—and fell hard, despite the red flags.

When her mother had a heart attack, Justine moved back to Melbourne and enrolled at Keiser University. She didn't expect to see Carl again, but he found her. At first, she was flattered. She helped him find an apartment. Then he convinced her to move in.

And that was when the scales began to tip.

Garden Party

Awakened by an ear-piercing buzzer, Justine sat up in her bunk. She dreamed of running through an open field, the wind in her hair — freedom. All she wanted was to drift back into that dream. But her first full day in prison was about to begin.

She didn't have a toothbrush, but Penny lent her some toothpaste. Justine dabbed it on her finger and scrubbed her teeth the best she could. Then they stood in line with their towels, waiting for the bathroom.

She studied herself in the shatterproof mirror. Two tired, empty eyes stared back.

The showers were lined against one wall — six heads in a row. Only a low partition offered any privacy. She was relieved the toilets, at least, had stalls. Perched on the cold metal bowl, she tried to stifle her sobs, not wanting anyone to witness her breakdown. To distract herself, she read the names etched into the cinderblock walls — women who had come and gone before her. Each name told a story. Somehow, it comforted her to know she wasn't the first to feel lost here.

Before breakfast, inmates stood outside their cubicles for roll call. Bunks had to be made military-style before heading to the cafeteria. Penny showed her the correct way to make her bed, neat and precise.

Justine's stomach growled, even though last night's dinner had left her queasy. *How bad could breakfast be?*

Inmates entered the cafeteria by security level. First came the administrative cases — segregated inmates with mental or emotional issues. Some carried on full conversations with invisible companions, eyes darting like wild animals. No one sat at their table.

Low- and medium-security inmates followed, most there for drug offenses, fraud, and parole violations. The high-security women came last. Their crimes were more violent: murder, armed assault.

Each table was ruled by its clique--Latinas at one, African Americans at another, older women clustered together, and lesbians at their own. Most of the inmates were Black or Hispanic. Justine wasn't prejudiced, but fear gripped her. Her upbringing had sheltered her from diversity. She had gone to an all-white, all-girls Catholic school. The only minorities she'd seen were in textbooks or TV dramas, and now those stereotypes swirled around her.

She moved cautiously through the serving line. A pretty woman with long, dark curls and almond-shaped eyes smiled and spooned hash browns onto her tray.

At the next station, Justine accidentally bumped into a heavyset Black woman.

"I'm so sorry," she said quickly.

"Next time, watch where you're going, Cracker!"

Justine recoiled, stunned. She stepped out of line and looked for a place to sit.

Sal, a heavy-set woman with a Southern accent, waved her over. "Saw what happened," she said. "That was Sharkesha. Level four. Don't get on her bad side. She's not right in the head." She tapped her temple. "Real short fuse."

"What's she in for?"

"Stabbed her husband while he slept. With his own hunting knife."

Justine's eyes widened. "Oh."

"Hey, Justine!" Penny called from across the room, waving. "Come sit with us!"

Relieved, Justine picked up her tray and joined her bunkmates. Stella was friendlier this morning.

"So," Stella said, "what's your story? How'd you land in paradise?"

"My boyfriend Carl planned a robbery. I was the getaway driver. He told me to wait in the car—I had no idea what he was up to."

"Join the club," Penny said. "I'm in here because of a man, too."

She was about to explain when a fight broke out in the food line.

"Hey! You can't cut in front of me!" a pale girl shouted.

"Who's gonna stop me?"

"That's Kendra," Stella whispered. "Always looking for a fight. Anger problems. Cindy's a fool for messing with her."

"What's Kendra in for?"

"Attempted murder. Beat up her best friend over crack. Eight years — flat time."

Before the guards could intervene, Kendra lunged, hands clamped around the blonde's neck. Two COs wrestled her off, dragging both women away.

Stella snorted. "Won't be seeing them for a while."

"Where are they taking them?" Justine asked.

"Not sure about the blonde, but Kendra's headed for solitary."

The fight cut breakfast short. Inmates were sent back to their pods or to their assigned work details.

"I'll tell you the rest of my sob story later," Penny said, grabbing her tray. "Laundry duty calls. See you at dinner."

Since it was Justine's first day, she was sent to the common room for orientation. Penny had warned her that, in the evenings, the women voted on what to watch on the one communal TV — usually something silly. Disagreements could get the TV turned off, and nobody wanted that. Today, though, the screen was off.

Justine sat on a hard plastic chair while the warden stood at the front and explained the prison rules, including how to address officers — *Officer*, *Mr.*, or *Ms.*

She was handed a list of rules:

- No access to other pods
- No sitting on someone else's bunk

- No hugging
- No sexual contact of any kind
- No spitting, biting, or throwing feces

Violations would result in solitary confinement or referral to the review board. Weapons of any kind were forbidden. "These rules," the warden said, "exist for the safety of the staff — and for yours."

Next, Justine received two forms: one for a list of approved visitors (maximum six), and another for the phone list, which had to be cleared by security. She listed only her mother and father. Her heart ached — she doubted her father wanted to speak to her. They hadn't spoken since the trial.

Her mother, though... Justine planned to use all her phone time calling her. They had once been close, until Justine's studies pulled her away from her mother's devout beliefs. Justine had thought herself smarter, more progressive. Now, she just felt ashamed.

At the end of orientation, they were handed a $20 commissary credit slip and a catalog of approved items — food, toiletries, even radios and TVs, though electronics required more funds. She thought about asking her father for money, but decided against it. *Maybe I could work in the laundry room with Penny.*

After orientation, they were marched to the medical unit for a physical exam and bloodwork.

Justine wasn't assigned to laundry, though. She was headed for the prison garden. *At least there'll be fresh air,* she thought.

Meatloaf

Justine and her three cellmates filed into the cafeteria for dinner. The air reeked of grease and disinfectant, hitting her like a wall of nausea.

"What's on the menu tonight?" she asked, wrinkling her nose.

"I think they call it meatloaf," Penny replied, grabbing a tray. "I call it mystery meat."

Justine chuckled. It was the first time she'd laughed all day.

After collecting their trays, they made their way to an empty table. Justine's gaze caught on a woman sitting alone at the far end of the room. She rocked slowly back and forth, her food untouched. Her arms were little more than sticks, and her eyes were hollow — as if she were slowly vanishing.

"Who's that?" Justine asked, lowering her voice.

"That's Tammy," Penny said. "She's on a hunger strike. Tried to hang herself with a sheet. They found her in time and stuck her in the loony ward, but it's full — so now she's back in gen pop."

"No one's helping her?"

"She's on suicide watch—admin case level. They're supposed to check on her every fifteen minutes. But you can see how that's going."

Justine looked away, her heart heavy. She took a bite of meatloaf, gagged, and spat it into her napkin.

"That's awful," she said, washing it down with lukewarm water.

Everyone at the table laughed.

She stuck to the overcooked vegetables, poking at them with her fork. "You never told me how you ended up here, Penny."

Penny sighed. "It's a dumb story. My husband turned our garage into a bomb shelter. Or so I thought. Turns out, it was a full-scale grow house—lights, fans, everything. I didn't ask questions. I had a kid to feed, and the bills were paid. The judge said I should've known. Gave me the mandatory minimum. Told me I was stupid."

"You're not stupid," Camila said softly. "You were just loyal."

Penny smiled faintly. "Thanks. But what did it get me? My boy's fourteen now. He'll be in high school before I'm out. My parents are raising him, thank God. He still looks up to me. But when he finds out the truth?" Her voice faltered. "That's what I'm really afraid of—losing him."

Penny looked at Justine. "What about Carl? Did they catch him?"

"Yeah. After three weeks on the run. He rolled over on his best friend and testified for a lighter sentence. Got four years. I got five for driving the car. My lawyer said I was lucky. Said under the new laws, I could've gotten fifteen."

Stella scoffed. "Sounds familiar. My boyfriend ran a whole drug ring — vacations, sports cars, the works. He gave me everything. One day, he asked me to mail a package for his cousin in California. Told me to use my name. Said they weren't speaking." She shook her head. "Turns out the box was full of Coke. He cut a deal, gave them my name, and walked. I had no clue what I was mailing."

"You can thank the war on drugs," Penny said. "Supposed to catch kingpins, but it crushes women like us. We take the fall while they make deals and get out early."

Justine pushed the food around on her tray. "If I'd had money for a real lawyer, maybe someone would've listened. But I got stuck with a public defender still wet behind the ears."

Camila, who'd been silent the whole time, finally spoke. Her voice was barely a whisper. "I didn't have a choice. I either helped Chico sell dope, or I got beaten. He didn't need much of a reason. His fists were always flying. He burned me with cigarettes." She rolled up her sleeves, showing the faded scars. "I had records from the women's shelter, but they wouldn't do anything unless I pressed charges. I was too scared."

She paused, eyes lowered.

"Then he made me rent a storage unit in my name. Said it was for furniture. I never even went there. Cops found drugs inside. They charged me."

"What happened?" Justine asked gently.

"My lawyer begged me to take a deal. Said I had no chance in the trial. I pleaded guilty. Got ten years. Chico got six — might be out in three."

"Criminal conspiracy," Penny muttered. "That's what they call it. We're all labeled collaborators. Judges love using us to set examples. It's their version of gender equality."

Stella frowned. "How do you know all this?"

"I read about it once — an article about women doing major time for minor roles. Nothing's changed."

"It's not fair," Camila whispered. "We carry the weight for their crimes. And they walk."

Justine slid her tray away, appetite gone.

"You gonna eat that meatloaf?" Stella asked.

"No." Justine pushed the tray toward her.

The dinner bell rang. Trays clattered as women rose and filed out of the cafeteria. Justine followed her cellmates back to the media room, but it was too noisy.

She went back to her cell and climbed to the top bunk, but her thoughts wouldn't quiet. From the hallway, the sound of a late-night comedy show buzzed faintly, followed by the guard's sharp laugh.

She imagined him with his feet on the desk, sipping Diet Coke, waiting for his next smoke break.

With a sigh, she pulled the thin pillow over her head and prayed for silence.

Peaches

The morning in the prison garden crawled, every weed pulled, and row tended, only reminding Justine how slowly time moved behind bars. Normally, she found peace in the earthy scent of soil and the quiet rustle of leaves, but today her thoughts were elsewhere. She kept glancing toward the clock tower, silently counting the minutes until she could head to the one place that offered real solace — the library.

While most inmates filed into the courtyard to gossip, smoke, or laze in the sun, Justine veered toward the modest brick building tucked behind the administration wing. The prison library wasn't much — just a few shelves of battered paperbacks and a legal section that had seen better days — but within those walls, there was silence, and in silence, purpose.

Justine buried herself in the law. Criminal conspiracy. Accomplice liability. Mandatory minimums. She devoured everything she could, trying to understand the very system that had swallowed her whole.

There was one computer in the corner, strictly for legal research. No saving. No printing. And certainly no internet. For everything else—journals, letters, motions—there was a clunky old typewriter that belonged in a museum. Most inmates gave up, defeated by tangled ribbons and stiff keys. But not Justine. She was determined to learn it.

Maryann, the librarian, was a soft-spoken woman with delicate features and a voice that always trembled, as if it were one breath away from breaking. She and Justine bonded quickly over their shared love of books—and their quiet defiance.

*****

One afternoon, Justine looked up from a thick volume on case law and caught Maryann wiping her eyes.

"What's wrong?" she asked gently.

Maryann hesitated, avoiding eye contact. Then, with a shaky breath, she said, "I just found out my father has cancer."

"Oh no. I'm so sorry."

Maryann wrung her hands, "I want to be with him before it's too late," she whispered. "But they won't grant me parole. Someone told me you studied law before you came here. Could you help me write a letter to the Parole Board?"

Justine nodded. "Of course. But what are you in for, if you don't mind me asking?"

Maryann lowered her voice. "Drug trafficking. My boyfriend—Larry—hid meth in the lining of my suitcase. We were flying to visit his brother in Italy. I didn't even know until we got stopped. He swore customs wouldn't find it, but the dogs did. I panicked. Tried to walk away, but they had me surrounded."

"What happened to him?"

"Nothing. The drugs were in my bag, not his. I took the fall."

Justine felt her jaw tighten. The story was too familiar. "I'll help you. You don't owe me anything."

Maryann offered a sad smile. "I don't have anything anyway. But... I do have a typewriter in my cell. You can have it. Might save you a few trips to the library."

That night, the clack of keys echoed softly in the cube as Justine typed beneath the dim bunk light.

"What are you doing?" Stella asked from the lower bunk.

"Helping Maryann write to the Parole Board."

Stella snorted. "Maryann's in for trafficking. You think a heartfelt letter's gonna undo that?"

"She's in the rehab program. Her father's dying. It might matter."

Stella shook her head. "The system doesn't reward good intentions. Especially not from jailhouse lawyers."

Justine said nothing. She knew Stella had a point — officials were quick to dismiss inmates who tried to outsmart the system. But this wasn't about Justine proving herself. It was about Maryann.

One morning in February, Maryann found her in the corridor. Her eyes were wide, rimmed with disbelief.

"You did it," she whispered. "They're letting me out."

"Really?"

"In time to be with my dad," Maryann said, tears welling. "I—I don't even have the words."

Justine smiled. "Then don't say anything. Just go."

For the first time since her sentencing, Justine felt something that resembled purpose. Even behind bars, she could still make a difference.

True to her word, Maryann gave her the typewriter. She also left a glowing note with the library staff, recommending Justine for the clerical position once the role reopened.

Camila had kept herself out of trouble and, with help from someone on the outside, managed to hire a new lawyer. Months later, she made parole.

They celebrated the only way they could—sharing stale snacks from the vending machine and laughing until lights-out. Justine was genuinely happy for her, though a quiet ache settled in her chest. Saying goodbye was bittersweet. For once, the system had worked in someone's favor, and it gave Justine a flicker of hope.

In true prison fashion, Camila insisted they play cards to determine who would inherit her belongings—a radio, a stash of ramen, a pair of flip-flops, and a well-worn hoodie. It was their way of keeping the mood light, of giving parting a sense of ceremony.

Within an hour of Camila's release, her bunk was filled again.

The new inmate introduced herself as Peaches—a broad-shouldered Black woman with labored breathing and wary eyes. She spoke little and kept mostly to herself, her presence quiet but watchful.

Justine didn't push. In prison, everyone had a story, but most were slow to tell it. Still, something about Peaches tugged at her—something beneath the silence, beneath the guarded expression and steady hands. She seemed like a woman who had learned to wear armor but never managed to heal the wounds beneath it.

Justine gave her space. But she also left an extra cup of coffee on the edge of Peaches's bunk the next morning—no questions asked, no expectations. Sometimes, kindness was the first step toward trust.

Legal Dynamics

As weeks turned into months, Justine began to navigate the complex legal dynamics of prison life. She grew into an advocate for fellow inmates. Some began calling her a "prison lawyer," a title that made her uneasy. She knew she still had much to learn. But the work gave her purpose — and a reason to keep going. Her growing desire to make things right, to help others who had been silenced or misrepresented, fueled her every step.

Word spread quickly. Inmates began seeking her out for help with appeals, parole hearings, sentence reductions, and formal complaints. They gave her a nickname — *Justice*. It started as a joke, but it stuck.

Justine found peace in the prison library. Sunlight streamed through a small, high window, a quiet reminder that summer still existed beyond the prison walls. She claimed a corner table and stacked it high with old law books. Much of the information was outdated, so she cross-checked it online using the single, heavily monitored computer reserved for legal research. No typing. No saving. No printing. Just access. It was slow and inefficient, but it was something.

One afternoon, she came across an article by law professor David L. Hudson, Jr., titled *Prisoner's Rights, Jailhouse Lawyers, and Access to Courts*. One passage struck her deeply:

"The Supreme Court invalidated a Tennessee prison rule that prohibited inmates from assisting others with legal matters, including preparing writs of habeas corpus, finding it denied many inmates access to the courts to file claims. Although rooted in due process, many later decisions characterize the Court's opinion as affirming that inmates retain the First Amendment right to petition the courts for a redress of grievances."

— *Johnson v. Avery* (1969), as discussed by David L. Hudson Jr.

Justine read the quote over and over. For the first time, she saw a legal precedent supporting what she was doing. She wasn't breaking rules — she was exercising a right.

Still, the guards watched her closely, waiting for a misstep. She couldn't have inmates lining up outside her cube — that would draw too much attention. Instead, she visited them in their pods, careful to keep her meetings brief.

One afternoon, as she stepped into a level-four block, a guard stopped her.

"What are you doing out of your pod, Justine?"

"I was visiting a friend."

"Unauthorized movement," he muttered, already scribbling on his clipboard. "You want ten days in solitary? You're not allowed in level four. I'm writing you up."

It was her second infraction in a month, both from the same officer. She kept her composure, but it stung. Thankfully, the guard was transferred to another building not long after.

The rest of the staff didn't seem as bothered. Some were even amused, shaking their heads as she passed with her arms full of books.

Justine didn't care. She had found something within those walls that gave her meaning. And for the first time since her sentencing, *Justice* wasn't just a nickname.

It was her mission.

*****

A few days later, a guard's voice bellowed into Justine's cube.

"Morgan! The warden wants to see you in his office. Now!"

Justine froze. Her gut clenched. *The transferred guard must've reported me before he left.*

She knocked gently on the warden's door.

"Come in," came the terse reply.

"Mr. Atwood, I was told you needed to see me."

He looked up, exhaling heavily as he raked his fingers through his short, graying hair. "Yes, Justine. Have a seat."

She did.

"I hear you've been acting as a jailhouse lawyer — and I don't like it. I know you studied some law on the outside, but that doesn't make you a lawyer. You have no formal credentials."

"With all due respect, Warden," she said carefully, "I'm not interfering with legal proceedings or giving legal advice. I help inmates draft letters to the parole board. That's their right. I'm not arguing cases — I'm helping them communicate clearly and professionally, based on what the review board looks for."

He studied her for a long moment, then sighed. "I realize you want to help, Justine. Just be careful. Not all guards will be as tolerant as I am."

She nodded, but she knew the risks. Even small acts of advocacy could lead to retaliation from staff. Still, she wasn't breaking the law. And she had precedent on her side.

Despite the warning, Justine continued to help inmates prepare letters for parole and clemency. She just worked more discreetly. The only place she felt truly safe was the prison chapel.

There were no stained-glass windows, but a single skylight spilled sunlight across the floor, giving the room a serene glow. A portrait of Jesus hung on the far wall — clad in robes of red and white — with the words: *"Jesus is our refuge and strength."*

The space reminded her of her last phone call with her mother.

"Don't turn your back on God, Justine. Spend time in the chapel. Revive your faith."

Justine sat alone in the front pew, waiting to meet a level-four inmate. She didn't know if she could help, but she agreed to listen.

When the woman finally walked in, Justine was surprised. She had expected someone big and hardened. Instead, a tiny woman approached hesitantly.

"Hi, are you Justine?"

"Yes."

"I'm Gail. Thank you for agreeing to meet me. I need your help."

"I'm not sure I can help," Justine replied, "but I'll try. Start at the beginning. Why did you stab your husband?"

Gail sat beside her, folding her hands. "Jim was a minister at King's Baptist Church. Everyone thought he was a godly man. The first time he hit me, he came home with flowers." Gail's eyes dropped to her lap. "Said he'd been praying for forgiveness. I believed him. I forgave him. But it happened again. And again. He'd find any excuse — if I wasn't home, if dinner was cold, or if I forgot to buy his favorite ice cream. I was so scared I hid a knife between the mattress and box spring — not to use, just to have something if things got bad."

"Didn't you have anyone to tell? At church? Family?"

"No one wanted to accuse *the minister*," she said softly. "He was charming. Charismatic. People adored him. Then a new girl started coming to Sunday service. A single mom. She saw right through me. She noticed the bruises under my veil. After a few weeks, she sat beside me and asked if someone was hurting me. I denied it, of course. Said I ran into a door. But she knew. Eventually, I told her everything. She'd been abused, too. We became friends."

"What happened?"

"Jim noticed. He thought we were getting too close. After one service, he ordered me home. Said he'd deal with me later.' I knew that meant a beating.

When he came in that night, I smelled liquor on his breath. He cursed the meal I made, saying it wasn't fit for a dog. Then he slapped me hard and told me to go upstairs.

"He followed me into the bedroom and struck me. I fell and hit the nightstand. My hand slid under the mattress, and I grabbed the knife I had hidden there. I stabbed him in the neck and shoulder. He was still fighting, still hitting me. I lost it and stabbed him again. I don't remember how many times. I blacked out. When I came to, blood was everywhere. I called the police and waited on the stoop. I've got ten years. If I make parole, I'll serve half and spend a year in a halfway house."

Justine's hands were clenched in her lap. "I've mostly helped women with drug cases," she said. "This will be a challenge. But perhaps we can build a case for self-defense. The abuse, the past police call, the pattern — it all matters."

Petitioning the court, though, was risky. This wasn't a parole letter. It was legal advocacy — and if the warden found out, Justine could land in serious trouble.

But looking at Gail—small, bruised, yet brave—Justine knew she had to try.

*****

After she met with Gail, Justine stayed in the chapel long after the woman had left, staring up at the small skylight as the sun filtered through. Dust particles floated in the still air like tiny spirits, catching the fading glow.

What am I doing? she wondered.

She hadn't come to prison to start a revolution. She hadn't even come with a plan. At first, she just wanted to survive. Then, helping others gave her purpose. But now? Now she was crossing lines—quiet ones drawn in pencil, easy to erase but hard to ignore. She knew prison politics. She knew that if the warden caught wind of her taking on Gail's case, it could cost her the clerical job, her library access, maybe even her parole.

She'd already gotten two write-ups.

Do I really want to risk being in solitary for someone I barely know?

She leaned forward, pressing her hands together like a prayer, though she wasn't sure who she was praying to. *Mom, you told me not to turn my back on God,* she thought. *But what if I'm not just turning my back on Him? What if I'm trying to play Him?*

Other inmates called her *Justice,* as if she could swoop in and make things right. Sometimes the nickname made her feel proud. Other times, it felt like a curse. She wasn't a lawyer. She didn't even finish undergrad. Her legal "expertise" was cobbled together from dated law books, online research, and desperation. What if she gave the wrong advice? What if someone lost their only chance at parole because of her?

You're not a lawyer, the warden had reminded her. She heard it on repeat in her head, like a gavel banging. *You have no formal training.*

Yet she also remembered Maryann—she smiled as she whispered, *"You did it. I'm going to be free."* That look of relief. That hope. Justine had given that to her.

And now Gail.

Gail's story haunted her—the bruises, the veil, the betrayal by the church, the police who laughed with her abuser. All Justine had ever done was drive a car. Gail had stabbed a man. *But wasn't that the same thing—reacting to someone else's crime?*

She thought of Carl. How he used her. How he walked away with a lighter sentence. *There's a pattern here,* she realized. *It's always the woman who pays.*

Still, she wasn't sure if she could carry the weight of someone else's justice. She already struggled under her own.

That night, she typed up notes from her conversation with Gail. Not on the library's computer—but on Maryann's old typewriter. Each key clicked loud and firm, like a tiny defiance against silence.

Halfway through her notes, she paused and whispered aloud, "I'm not trying to be a lawyer. I'm just trying to help."

But even as she said it, she felt the tension in her chest, that creeping fear. If she went too far, the system would push back. And it wouldn't be gentle.

She stared at the unfinished page in the typewriter and sat back in her chair, hands hovering over the keys.

Who do I want to be in here? A helper? A rule-breaker? A fraud? Or maybe… just someone trying to make amends.

She didn't know the answer yet. But the next morning, when she walked past the chapel, she slipped inside, sat in the front pew, and whispered a simple prayer:

"God, if I'm wrong, stop me. But if I'm right… Give me the strength to keep going."

Lily White

Justine felt the urge to use the toilet, but decided to return to her pod first to grab a fresh uniform and her toiletries. A hot shower was calling her. She stepped into the corridor, already imagining the steam on her face — only to stop short.

A sudden commotion outside her cubicle made her pulse quicken.

Her heart lurched when she saw a guard carrying her typewriter down the hallway.

"That's mine!" she shouted, rushing toward him.

The guard didn't even glance her way.

"I didn't steal it!" she cried, panic rising like bile in her throat.

"Hands on your head!" a sharp voice barked.

She turned to see a man in a black uniform — not DOC blue. Across the back of his vest, bold white letters spelled DEA.

"Eyes on the ground!" he yelled, spittle flying from his mouth.

Justine's breath caught. She obeyed, her body shaking as he roughly grabbed her wrists and snapped cold steel cuffs around them.

"Where are you taking me?" she asked, her voice cracking.

"You're going to the hole."

"What? Why?" she pleaded, her mind racing, Stella's voice echoing in her memory — *The system doesn't reward women for trying to better themselves.*

Her bladder screamed.

"Do I have time to pee?" she asked desperately.

The guard sneered. "Oh, don't worry. You'll pee soon enough. Now move!"

They marched her to the isolation pod. A female officer performed a cold, clinical strip search and handed her a plastic cup for a urine sample. No explanations. No answers.

Afterward, they led her down to the lowest level of the building. The air turned damp and frigid. Echoes of screams and sobbing bounced off the cinderblock walls. Justine flinched at the sound of a woman pounding on a door. Another voice murmured a prayer.

Cells lined the corridor like forgotten tombs. She was shoved into one — six feet by six, a metal toilet, a sink, a cot bolted to the wall. The door had a narrow slot for food trays and handcuffs.

The cell swallowed her.

Justine sat on the cot and sobbed into the flat, mildewed pillow. The damp stench clung to her skin, mixing with the sweat and dirt still on her body from garden duty. She hadn't showered. She hadn't peed. Her body ached with humiliation and the sharp injustice of it all.

Was this punishment for helping? For being visible? For trying to change something?

She curled into herself, desperate to sleep, to shut it all out. But there was no peace in the hole.

The voices from other cells never stopped — pleading, ranting, singing in cracked voices, arguing with ghosts. There was no sense of time. In her pod, the lights shut off at ten. Here, they stayed on. A cold fluorescent hum washed everything in sterile brightness, erasing night and day.

She stared at her dirt-caked fingers.

I should've gone straight to the showers, she thought bitterly. *I didn't even get to pee.*

*****

When the narrow window in the steel door slid open with a metallic scrape, Justine jumped up and rushed to it.

"Please," she called out, her voice cracking. "I need to take a shower."

The guard didn't answer. The window slammed shut.

Justine slid down the wall, the cold concrete pressing through her thin uniform. She buried her face in her hands and wept, her sobs muffled by the stale air.

Then, from somewhere above, a voice floated through the vent.

"Hey... Justine? That you?"

She looked up, startled. "Stella?"

"Yeah, it's me. You okay?"

"I—I don't know. What's going on? Why are we even in here?"

"There was a sweep. DEA stormed in this morning and pulled everyone out of their cubes. Next thing I knew, they were hauling us to seg."

"Seg?" Justine repeated.

"Segregation," Stella said flatly. "Lockdown. Isolation. Whatever you wanna call it."

"But why?"

"Drugs. Someone tipped them off. Said contraband was moving through our pod."

Justine's heart dropped. "You think... it was Peaches?"

"I don't know," Stella said, her voice harder now. "But it doesn't matter. Most of the women in here are in on drug charges. That makes us all suspects. Some come in still using and find ways to stay high. They hide things. Trade for favors. Sell each other out."

"That's insane. Why would they do that?"

"Because they're addicts," Stella replied. "Because they'll do anything for a hit. Some offer sex to guards for pills or powder. Others rat people out just to curry favor with COs. They get off on the chaos. They live for it."

Justine leaned her head against the wall, the cement sucking away her warmth. "How long do you think we'll be here?"

"Depends. It could be days — could be weeks. My friend Tina? She was here for almost a month. Said she got to shower twice, maybe. One hour outside, in a cage with nothing but a bench. She said it made her feel like a dog."

"What happened to her?"

Stella hesitated. "She was granted parole. I was supposed to go home in two days. Then she got into a fight with Sherry — you know, the one who always looks like she's ready to snap? Sherry didn't like seeing anyone get out. She sabotaged her."

Justine sat up straighter. "How?"

"It was movie night. Tina tried to sit in the only open chair — next to Sherry. Sherry blocked her. Tina called her a bitch and walked away. But Sherry jumped her. Pulled a sharpened toothbrush and swung. Tina shoved her, and it ended up in Sherry's shoulder. Next thing you know, they're both in seg. Tina lost parole."

Justine was about to respond when shouting erupted across the hall.

"Get your filthy hands off me, you piece of shit!"

Boots pounded the floor. A door slammed. Then — banging. Fists or feet or both, hammering against steel.

"Let me out of here! I have COPD! I can't breathe!"

Justine gasped. "Stella... do you hear that? That sounds like Peaches."

She raised her voice. "Peaches? Is that you?"

The banging stopped. A few seconds passed.

"Yeah," came the hoarse reply. "It's me. Justine?"

"I'm here. And Stella's in the next cell."

"Stella?" Peaches repeated, her voice sharper now.

"Yeah, I'm here," Stella snapped. "Was it you that got us locked up in here, you stupid bitch?"

"You're only saying that because I'm Black," Peaches shot back, raw and bitter.

"No," Stella replied coldly. "It's because you love drugs."

Silence.

Then Peaches said, quieter but with venom, "Well, I've got news for you. Your lily-white friend Penny was the one using. I saw her."

Justine froze. "Penny? No. She wouldn't. She's trying to get back to her son. That would ruin everything."

"You're living in a fantasy world, Justine," Peaches said, voice hollow now. "Wake up. Nobody's who they pretend to be in here."

Vultures

Justine had another sleepless night. The sterile glow of the lights never dimmed, but it was a comfort to know Stella was close. They sat on the floor by their respective vents, whispering for hours through the grate in the wall — two voices in the dark trying to make sense of the senseless.

"How did she even get the drugs?" Justine asked.

"I don't know," Stella murmured. "They screen everything that comes in. There's really only one way — a crooked guard."

That night, Justine dreamed of her mother. She appeared like an angel, dressed in a flowing white gown, her face radiant, her voice soft as harp music echoed in the background.

"I'll always love you," her mother whispered.

It was so beautiful that Justine reached out to touch her, but her mother floated away on a cloud, fading from view.

She woke with a jolt, disoriented. For a split second, she forgot where she was. Then reality struck like a punch to the chest. The cold walls. The toilet in the corner. The stale air.

Her chest tightened. She couldn't breathe.

The days blurred. Time ceased to move. She counted meals to track the hours. She barely touched the food — the bread was stiff, the meat sour. She felt hollow, both from hunger and from the slow erosion of her spirit.

Then one morning, the metal latch clanged open.

Justine flinched. It wasn't time for her hour outside.

"Put your hands out, Morgan," the guard barked.

She slid her arms through the slot. He fastened the cuffs, opened the door, and motioned her out.

"Move it."

"Where are you taking me?" she asked, her voice thin with hope and dread.

"Back to population."

A wave of relief washed through her. "Am I going back to my cube?"

"No. You've been reassigned. Check in at your pod for your new cubicle."

"What about my stuff?"

He shrugged.

At the pod, she approached the desk and asked about her belongings. A guard handed her a trash bag containing a uniform and a scuffed pair of boots.

"Where are my toiletries?" she asked.

"This is all we have," he said flatly.

"Someone stole my things!"

"I guess you'll have to get new ones now, won't you?"

Before she could respond, another voice intervened — Officer Jenkins.

"I'm sorry," he said, his tone sincere. "When inmates know someone's not coming back, sometimes they ransack the cube. Visitation's on Saturday. Maybe someone can bring you what you need."

"Thank you, Officer Jenkins." It was the first kindness she'd felt in days. "Also... I had an old typewriter. A guard took it during the sweep."

Jenkins frowned. "We could file a claim, but to be honest, you probably won't see it again." He handed her a form. "Fill this out anyway."

She nodded. "Thanks."

Back in the pod, she found Stella just two cubes down. But Penny was gone.

A knot formed in Justine's stomach.

At least she recognized one of her new cellmates — Sara, the petite girl from the cafeteria line. Sara had the bunk above Justine now. She was so tiny, Justine sometimes worried the mattress might swallow her whole.

"Who else is in here?" Justine asked, trying to settle her nerves.

"Doris is on the bottom bunk across from us. Amy's above her."

"Doris — the one from Brooklyn who's always fighting?"

Sara giggled. "Yeah, but she's harmless. Funny as hell, actually."

"If you say so. And Amy?"

"Probation violator. She won't be here long. It's just a scare tactic."

"Where is she now?"

Sara tilted her head toward the common area. "Probably playing cards."

Justine was assigned a lower bunk this time. She collapsed onto it, pulled the thin sheet over her head, and cried softly, releasing the weight of solitary one tear at a time.

Later, she approached a guard to request phone access.

"You'll have to check with the warden," he said. "But I'm sure he'll allow it. You just got out of the hole."

As she passed the common area, she spotted a circle of women playing cards.

"Raise," said a woman with platinum hair and dark roots.

"I'll pass," muttered another.

"Call."

"Full house," the platinum-haired woman announced with a smug grin, slapping her cards down.

"Who's Amy?" Justine asked.

The woman looked her over. "Who wants to know?"

"I'm Justine. Your new cellmate."

"You play?"

"Sometimes. Crazy Eights."

"Then have a seat. We'll teach you poker."

"I'd love to," Justine said with a smile, "but I'm headed to the warden's office."

"What, in trouble already?"

"Not this time," she said and walked off.

At the warden's office, she knocked softly.

"Come in," came the voice from inside.

Mr. Atwood looked up from his paperwork. "Morgan. You all right?"

"Not really," she said. "I thought I was thrown in solitary for helping women write parole letters. But I heard it was because of drugs. I'm confused. And… Penny's gone."

His expression darkened. "She's been indicted for trafficking drugs inside the prison. Got too cozy with a guard. She's been transferred to a facility in Tennessee."

Justine blinked. "Penny? But… she talked about her son all the time. She said she was wrongly arrested."

"She might've believed it," Atwood said. "Doesn't matter. They all claim innocence. It's part of the dance."

"It should matter," Justine insisted. "Maybe if there were more programs — more education — these women would have a reason to fight for something better."

He sighed and leaned back in his chair. "This place changes people. Not always for the better."

"But hope changes people, too. If the college partnered with the facility again —"

"No one wants to invest in prisoners," he said, voice low. "For every one we let go, two more walk in. It's a machine."

"Even machines can be rewired."

He studied her for a moment. "You're a dreamer, Morgan."

She smiled. "Maybe. But I'd rather dream than rot."

He chuckled faintly, reached for his pen. "Persistent, I'll give you that." He scribbled something on a slip and handed it to her. "Take this to the office — they'll open a phone line for you."

He rummaged in a drawer and held out a toothbrush. "Best I can do. You'll have to buy your own toothpaste."

"Thank you, Mr. Atwood."

He nodded and returned to his paperwork.

Justine left the office holding the permission slip and toothbrush, like small victories.

Rehabilitation

Penny was the only inmate Justine had truly trusted. What went wrong?

She kept replaying the signs she'd missed—the subtle deflections, the way Penny avoided the rehab program. Justine had thought it was pride, or fear of judgment. But now it was clear: Penny hadn't avoided rehab because she thought she didn't need it. She'd avoided it because she was using. The addiction had won.

No matter how much she'd talked about her son, about rebuilding her life, in the end, it hadn't been enough.

Maybe Stella knows more, Justine thought.

She walked down the corridor and stopped at Stella's cube.

"Hi," she said softly. "Do you have a minute?"

Stella closed her book—the same one she'd been pretending to read all week—and gave a small nod. "Sure. What's on your mind?"

"It's Penny." Justine hesitated. "I can't stop thinking about her. I just... don't understand. Why would she throw away her chance to get out? Did you know she was using?"

Stella exhaled slowly. "I suspected. But in here? You learn to stay out of other people's business. It's how you survive."

"Maybe she just... lost hope." Justine's voice was barely audible. "Do you know who runs the rehab program?"

Stella squinted at her. "Oh no. I know that look. You're about to stir up some shit. What are you planning now?"

"Nothing bad," Justine said quickly. "I just... maybe if I sat in on the program, I'd learn how it works. Maybe figure out why some women drop out — or never join to begin with."

"You really think they'll let you make changes?" Stella said, half-laughing. "They don't like questions, and they *hate* paperwork. Besides, you don't know what's wrong with the program yet."

"Exactly. That's why I want to go through it myself."

Stella snorted. "Camila did — and she wasn't even an addict. Guess anyone can sign up if they want to."

"Then I'm signing up."

Stella shook her head, half amused. "Girl, you've got too much time on your hands. Let's eat before all the vaguely edible food is gone."

They made their way through the chow line. As they sat down, Stella nodded toward the far end of the room.

"Look. Peaches. Back from the hole. Word is she flipped out bad. They've got her on admin-level now."

Justine followed her gaze. Peaches looked... different. Quieter. Smaller somehow.

"She's not doing well," Justine murmured.

"She needed to lose a few pounds anyway," Stella said, stabbing her food. "She's always eating off other people's trays."

"Why don't you like her?"

Stella shrugged. "I don't know. Maybe we got off on the wrong foot."

Just then, Peaches shuffled over, her shoulders hunched, eyes dull.

"Mind if I sit?" she asked, her voice subdued.

Justine looked at Stella, who hesitated, then gestured to the empty seat.

"Sure," Stella said. "Why not?"

Peaches lowered herself slowly into the chair.

"What happened?" Justine asked. "Why weren't you released with us?"

"Anxiety," Peaches said flatly. "I panicked. Said some things. Pissed off the wrong guard. They kept me longer. This place — it's full of sadists."

Justine tread carefully. "Not all of them. Officer Jenkins seems fair."

Peaches scoffed. "For every Jenkins, there are three guards who abuse their power. Verbal. Physical.

Sexual. And most women here are too scared to say a word."

"I still believe most of them are just doing their jobs," Justine said, trying to stay neutral. "They've got families, too."

"If you say so." Peaches glanced at Justine's tray. "Hey — you gonna eat that?"

Justine slid her unopened dessert across the table. "Go ahead."

Then she stood. "Rehab starts in ten. I want to be on time."

Stella gave her a smirk. "Grrr. Get 'em, tiger."

But Justine didn't head straight there. Instead, she found a quiet bench by the window in the common area and sat with her thoughts.

The background chatter of card games and clinking trays faded into a low hum as her mind drifted to Penny.

Penny, with her nervous laugh and soft voice, whenever she talked about her son. Penny, who once clutched his school photo like it was the last tangible piece of love she had left. Penny, who hummed to herself on her bunk, pretending life still had rhythm.

Justine had believed in her. Believed that maternal love could be a lifeline. That it could anchor someone. Pull them back from the edge.

But it hadn't.

Maybe Penny had lost faith that she'd ever see her son again. Maybe the prison system had chipped away at her until she stopped fighting. Maybe the day she said yes to a fix, she wasn't thinking of anything but getting through the next hour.

Justine felt the weight of it settle into her chest.

I should've seen it. Should've said something. Should've pushed her to get help.

But deep down, she knew: no one could force someone to fight their own demons. Not if they weren't ready.

Penny hadn't been strong — she'd just been good at pretending. She was surviving, not living. Hiding behind soft smiles and bedtime stories about a little boy who still thought she was a hero.

Now she was gone. Transferred. Reduced to another cautionary tale.

Justine wiped her eyes. Maybe Stella was right. Maybe she *was* a dreamer. But she couldn't let Penny's story end in silence.

She was going to that rehab program — not just to sit through it, but to *understand* it. To see where it failed. To see if it could be salvaged. Because if even one woman could be saved from slipping the way Penny had, it would matter.

She would carry Penny's story with her like a folded letter — faded but sacred. Quiet but urgent.

Because for every woman who gave up, someone had to keep trying.

Someone like her.

Strip Search

Justine stepped quietly into the chapel, where the prison's drug rehabilitation program was held. The altar had been cleared to make space for eight plastic chairs arranged in a circle, the stained-glass windows casting fractured light over the floor. She slipped into a back pew and watched in silence.

At the front stood Mr. Harris, a stocky man in his mid-fifties, his posture weary but authoritative. He paced slowly, lecturing about cognitive distortions and the mental traps that fueled addiction. In the circle, a young woman with long blond braids rocked back and forth in her seat, eyes unfocused, disconnected from the conversation.

"Hailee," Mr. Harris said, turning toward her, "can you name any thoughts or emotions that led you to substance abuse?"

Hailee stilled. "When I'm under stress," she said softly, "I crave getting high."

"And how might she handle that stress in a healthier way?" he asked the group.

A plain-looking woman to her left raised her hand. "She could remove herself from the situation. Go for a walk."

"Perfect, Kathy. That's a great example."

"Oh, please," scoffed Elena, her voice edged with cynicism. "In my neighborhood, husbands killed their wives, junkies murdered people, and prostitutes got beaten in the street. Nobody cared. Nobody came."

"She can leave — in her head," Kathy replied.

"What does that mean?" Nancy asked, folding her arms.

"It means she can choose not to react," Kathy said gently. "Mentally check out. Tune out the chaos."

"She could try breathing exercises," another woman added. "Or listen to music."

Stephanie giggled nervously. "Sometimes it's just easier to give in."

"You have to fight the craving," Elena snapped.

"I don't know how," Stephanie murmured, her voice trembling.

"I've beaten addiction," said a red-faced woman with blotchy skin. "But it's a lonely road. Don't expect help from people who want to keep you down. Misery loves company."

"I didn't mean to get hooked," Nancy said. "My boyfriend pressured me into doing coke. When I said no, he said I was stuck-up, trying to make him look bad. I just... didn't want to lose him."

"Do you have trouble saying no?" Elena asked, her tone pointed.

Nancy shrugged. "It's hard. When we were high, we had fun. Thinking about it still makes my heart race."

"It's not easy to resist cocaine," Mr. Harris interjected. "But you have to recondition your thinking. Weigh the short-term high against the long-term damage — lost jobs, broken families, ruined health."

"I've tried," Hailee whispered. "But I always find a reason to relapse."

"Then you need to avoid the triggers," he said gently.

"My whole life is a trigger," she replied bitterly. "My environment. My people. Everything."

"I drank for ten years," said Veronica. "Told myself I was just social. Until I hit a kid on a bike. That ended that lie. But it was already too late."

"There's no hope," the girl with the braids muttered.

Veronica whipped around. "Oh, now you talk? Don't dump your gloom on us."

"There's always hope," Mr. Harris said, trying to diffuse the tension.

"You can't change if you're still hanging around the same people," Elena insisted.

Nancy glared. "Miss Guatemala thinks she knows everything. So why's she still here?"

That did it.

A Black woman shot to her feet. "What, your shit don't stink? You're just another addict like the rest of us."

Mr. Harris raised his hand. "That's enough. We're done for today. Same time next Tuesday."

As the group dispersed, Justine stood and approached.

"Mr. Harris? Could I speak with you a moment?"

He looked up, wary. "And you are?"

"Justine Morgan. I'd like to join the program."

"Are you an addict?"

"No," she said. "But someone I cared about was. She wouldn't come here, and I didn't understand why. I want to know. Maybe if I had, I could've helped her."

He studied her. "We can't force inmates to participate. And we don't waste time on those who aren't serious."

"Then offer incentives," Justine said. "Credits for good behavior. Early release to a halfway house."

His jaw tightened. "Every so often, someone comes in here trying to game the system. I don't know your angle, and frankly, I don't want to."

"I'm not gaming anything," she said. "I just want to help."

"That's part of the problem," he muttered. "People outside this room want reform. People inside want punishment. We walk a razor's edge between both."

"I know most of these women are here because of drugs," she said. "And I know you're doing your best. But if there was more hope, maybe fewer would relapse. Maybe fewer would come back."

He sighed, his shoulders sinking. "It's a noble idea. But it's also unrealistic. Budgets are tight. We barely have the resources to run what we've got."

"There has to be a better way."

He looked at her for a long moment. "You mentioned classes?"

"Something creative. Self-awareness. Meditation. Even sewing or cooking. Things that build confidence. Things that engage."

He considered her for a beat longer, then gave a slow nod. "Fine. You can sit in. But if we try any of your ideas, you're organizing them."

Justine smiled. "Deal. Thank you."

He handed her a clipboard. "Fill out this intake form. You start next week."

She clutched it to her chest like a key.

For the first time since Penny's transfer, she felt like maybe something could change after all.

Even here.

Holiday Blues

Justine flopped onto her bunk and reached for a library book, eager to lose herself in someone else's story. Before she could even open the cover, a guard poked his head into the cell.

"Morgan, you've got a visitor."

"Me? Are you sure?"

The guard raised a brow. "Do you want the visit or not?"

She scrambled to her feet, heart suddenly racing. Her mother wasn't strong enough for the long drive. *Had something happened?*

Her stomach twisted as she followed the guard down the corridor toward the visitor conference room.

Inside sat a man she didn't recognize — early forties, dark hair, piercing blue eyes, clean-cut in a navy suit. He stood when she entered.

"Justine Morgan?"

"Yes," she said cautiously.

"I'm Blake Sullivan. Your new attorney."

She stared at him, stunned. "Attorney?"

"Your father hired me."

Her breath caught. "My... father?" Her voice cracked. "He paid for a lawyer?"

Blake nodded. "He reached out a few weeks ago. I've already filed a motion for appeal."

Her heart pounded. "An appeal?" She leaned forward. "That's real? Like... the appellate court reviews the case? They check if everything was done fairly?"

"It's a long shot," he said, honest but calm. "But yes. The appellate court is the first step. If that fails, we can explore federal remedies."

"Isn't that... expensive?"

"He's covering it."

Justine's breath wavered. It was the first meaningful gesture she'd received from her father — maybe ever. For a moment, she didn't know whether to cry or laugh.

"It could take eighteen months," Blake added gently. "Sometimes longer. You'll have to be patient."

She nodded slowly. "Thank you. Really. Thank you."

They shook hands. His grip was warm, steady. Something about it settled into her like a quiet promise.

After the visit, she endured another strip search and was escorted back to her pod. But this time, the cold stare from the guard didn't faze her. Her skin still tingled — not from embarrassment, but from the touch of possibility.

She sat back on her bunk, the book still unopened in her lap. But she didn't need to escape into fiction anymore.

For the first time in a long time, she felt something real.

Hope.

*****

Justine didn't want to be negative, but three weeks had passed. Still no word from Blake, her new lawyer.

Maybe everyone's on break for the holidays, she told herself, though the excuse rang hollow.

Christmas in prison was a dull echo of the real thing. The turkey was cold, the stuffing dry—likely powdered from a box. The guards, unusually hands-off, kept to themselves, holed up in the staff room with their catered meals, pretending not to notice the inmates' restless energy. Meanwhile, the women picked at their trays under flickering lights and forced small talk over lukewarm food.

Justine collected her tray and scanned the room. Some tables buzzed with tense laughter. Others simmered in silence. Near the window sat a woman in her sixties, thin and rigid, her gaze locked on the gray sky. Her stillness was unsettling—hollow, yet alert.

Justine walked over. "Mind if I sit here?"

The woman didn't turn. "Did they send you to commit me?"

"No. I just wanted to check in. See how you're doing."

Slowly, the woman turned her head. Her eyes were pale and cloudy, but her stare cut sharp. "You're looking at me like I'm crazy. They got to you, didn't they?"

"I'm an inmate," Justine said gently. "Same as you."

The woman turned back to the window. "I hate Christmas."

Justine didn't reply. She just waited.

"It was during the hospital Christmas party," the woman said, her voice low and oddly detached. "I starved myself for five days. Got my hair done, full makeup, new red dress. Tight, but tasteful. I wanted Peter to notice me. I wanted to feel beautiful again."

She let out a bitter laugh. "He didn't even glance at me. Said he was tired. Spent the night staring at a table of nurses. One of them stared back—a blonde in a black dress two sizes too small. Her tits were practically falling out. By the end of the night, they were dancing. I knew then. She was going to steal my husband."

Her eyes gleamed. "There should be penalties for women who go after married men. Don't you think?" She turned abruptly. "Are you married?"

"No," Justine said. "I had a boyfriend. It ended badly."

"They always do," the woman muttered. "Peter and I were high school sweethearts. I worked two jobs while he was in med school. Never complained. When he opened his practice, I stayed home to raise our boys.

I ironed his shirts. I baked cupcakes for the PTA. I was a good wife."

Her voice cracked with rage. "Then he started calling me names — stupid cow, useless bitch. I told myself he was stressed. That it would pass." She locked eyes with Justine. "He gaslit me for years. Told me I imagined things. That I was unstable."

Justine shifted. This wasn't just a conversation — it was a confession, unraveling one word at a time.

"After thirty years of marriage, he asked for a divorce. Gave everything to her — the house, the boat, the retirement accounts. Left me with nothing but our boys."

She paused, breathing shallowly. "And then... he turned them against me, too. Weekend visits became Disneyland. I couldn't compete. Of course, they chose him."

Her lip trembled, but the tears didn't come. "If he was two minutes late dropping them off, I'd drive to his house. Cops always showed up. He said I was violating a restraining order."

"Couldn't you fight it?" Justine asked quietly.

Helena let out a laugh — sharp and jagged. "Fight who? A respected doctor? My friends thought I'd lost it. 'Poor Helena — must be menopause.' No one believed me."

Justine swallowed. "What about your children?"

"He poisoned them. Turned me into the villain in my own story." Her hands clenched the edge of the table, knuckles bloodless. "I was a good mother. I stayed. I showed up."

She drew in a breath, shaky but controlled. "They wanted me to crack. Hang myself. But I didn't."

Justine's voice was barely a whisper. "What did you do?"

Helena turned. Her voice was cold, smooth, terrifying in its clarity.

"I shot them. Him and her. Point blank."

Silence dropped like a curtain. Justine sat, staring into Helena's eyes—and saw something behind them shift. A reel that never stopped playing.

"I'm not sorry," Helena said.

Justine rose slowly. "Well... I should get back to my table."

Helena didn't reply. She turned back to the window, eyes locked on something far beyond the concrete walls.

"Merry Christmas," Justine said softly, the words brittle and useless.

Helena didn't look up.

Winter White

Winter had shut down the garden, and Justine didn't yet have a new job assignment. With nothing to do, she walked past the armed guard and stood at the courtyard gate, waiting to join the other inmates on the patio. The frigid air burned her lungs and escaped her mouth in misty clouds. It was below freezing, but she preferred the cold. The wind slapped her cheeks until they went numb—not a bad feeling, all things considered. Out here, she didn't feel as confined, except for the rows of gleaming razor wire that crowned the fences. The patio was the only place where she felt something close to free.

A guard called her name. "Morgan, Mr. Harris wants to see you."

Her heart fluttered. *It has to be about the class proposal.*

She smiled to herself as she entered Mr. Harris's office.

"Great news," he said, beaming. "I spoke with the warden. He approved your idea to start classes. Just one to begin with. I think we should make it meditation-based—something to calm the savage beasts."

Justine chuckled politely. "That's great. I heard one of the women in our pod practices yoga. Maybe I can recruit her to lead it."

"All right," he said, but raised a finger. "Limit it to ten inmates. I don't want this getting out of hand."

"I understand. A lot of the women will be thrilled. If it goes well, maybe we can add Pilates."

Mr. Harris grinned. "You're pushy—I'll give you that. Happy New Year, Morgan."

"Happy New Year."

Justine headed straight for Becky—the quiet girl always folded into some impossible shape, humming softly like she belonged to a different realm. She found her in her cube, sitting cross-legged in a lotus position. A thin, woven blanket was all that separated her from the cold concrete floor.

"Hi, Becky?"

Becky opened her eyes slowly, looking at Justine like she'd appeared in a dream.

"Sorry to bother you," Justine said.

"You're not." Her voice was light, calm. "Aren't you that girl they call Justice?"

"Yeah… that's me." Justine smiled nervously. "I was wondering—would you be interested in guiding a yoga class for some of the inmates?"

Becky's expression clouded. "Teach? I can't *teach*. Yoga has to come from within."

"Okay, not teach exactly. More like... lead. Or guide. What about meditation? I think it would help a lot of these women with their stress."

"No." Becky shook her head sharply. "Some of these women have deep-seated anger. They'd break the healing spell. I can't risk that. I can't put myself in danger."

Justine softened her voice. "It's okay. I didn't mean to upset you."

Becky looked to the ceiling, her voice suddenly ethereal. "The gods forgive you... So I will, too."

Justine turned to leave, then paused. "By the way... what's *Om*?"

Becky raised her hand in a fluid motion, as if brushing the question into the air. "Om is the seed of all sound in the universe. People think it's one syllable, but it's actually three — A-U-M. It's sacred. Chanting can bring peace."

"Thanks," Justine said, genuinely curious now. "I always wondered."

"And just so you know," Becky added, "meditation originated from Buddhism. Here." She reached behind her and handed Justine a small, creased book. "You can read about it if you like. But bring it back."

"Do you have a book on yoga, too?"

Becky sifted through a small stack of paperbacks and produced one with frayed corners and hand-drawn diagrams. "Here."

"Thank you." Justine took the books and headed back to her cube, the disappointment setting in.

Amy was reading on her bunk, and Doris sat on a stool, filing her nails.

"I can't believe it," Justine said. "I finally got the warden to approve classes, and Becky refuses to teach yoga."

"Forget her," Amy muttered without looking up. "She's bat-shit crazy anyway."

"Do you know anyone else who could lead a meditation or yoga session?"

"Nope."

"You might have to do it yourself," Doris offered, waving her plastic file like a wand. "You look like one of those suburban yoga girls. I bet you belonged to a fitness club."

"Yeah, I took a class or two at the gym, but I don't know much about all that Zen stuff."

Amy looked up. "You're good at writing letters, right? Why not reach out to a yoga circle? See if someone wants to take on a prison reform project."

"That's actually a great idea." Justine perked up. "I'll handwrite the letters on the commissary stationery. My typewriter was never returned."

Without access to the computer, Justine turned to the ancient prison copy of the Yellow Pages. The spine was cracked, and most pages were loose or missing, but she flipped through until she found a few listings for local fitness centers and yoga studios. There was no telling if they were still open.

Dear Yoga Instructor,

My name is Justine Morgan, and I'm currently an inmate at Larsen Correctional Institute for Women. I've recently been granted approval to start a yoga class here, something I believe could bring a sense of calm and healing to many women in this facility.

I had hoped to find someone inside willing to lead the class, but so far, no one feels confident enough to take on that responsibility. That's why I'm reaching out in the hope that someone from the outside might extend compassion to a group of women who have very few outlets for their stress and anxiety.

If you or someone you know would be open to volunteering or even offering guidance remotely, it could make a real difference.

Thank you for taking the time to consider this request.

With gratitude,
Justine Morgan

Yoga

Justine mailed out the letters and waited. In the meantime, she studied the book Becky had given her, practicing breathing techniques and simple poses in her cell. If no one responded, Plan B was to teach the class herself — even if the thought made her nervous.

A few weeks later, she was sitting cross-legged on her bunk, reading about the Eight Limbs of Yoga, when the PA system crackled overhead.

"Mail call!" the guard barked, sparking a flurry of inmates rushing toward the pod entrance.

"Justine," he shouted.

Her heart jumped. She scrambled to her feet, met the guard, and took the white envelope from his hand.

"It's from a yoga studio!" she said, her fingers already tearing it open.

A small crowd gathered around her.

"Well? What does it say?" Amy asked, peering over her shoulder.

Justine unfolded the letter and read aloud.

Dear Justine,

I was excited to receive your letter. I would love to do my part.

Have you heard of the Prison Yoga Project? They believe that people who are committed to self-awareness can turn their lives around. If I can alleviate anyone's suffering in any way, I will gladly take the time to teach.

I've already received authorization from the board of prisons. I'm sending the paperwork today.

Sincerely,
Jill St. Claire

P.S. Make sure everyone who wants to participate brings a towel to sit on.

Cheers and claps erupted around her.

"I hope you girls are going to support the program," Justine said, holding the letter like it was made of gold.

"Why should I join yoga?" Doris asked, folding her arms. "I'm in for life. Besides, I'm not into that spiritual stuff."

Justine gave her a pointed look. "Can't you think about the bigger picture? If this works, maybe the warden will let us have more creative classes — writing, art, music — real programs."

Doris sighed dramatically. "Fine. I'll come. But only because it's you, Justine."

"Thank you," Justine said, grinning. "Who knows? You might actually enjoy it. You could be the next prison yogi."

Doris rolled her eyes. "Geez. Namaste or whatever."

*****

Jill St. Claire arrived at the prison a month later, escorted to the recreation room.

Justine had expected someone a bit more "hippy" — maybe like Stephanie or Becky. But Jill was petite, with curly brown hair, clear olive skin, and soulful eyes that immediately put her at ease.

"Are you Justine?" Jill asked, her words lightly laced with a French accent.

"Yes. You must be Jill. I really appreciate you coming. Most people are too scared."

Jill laughed. "I'm not worried."

"Are you French?"

"No, Italian. St. Claire is my married name — my husband's French. I'm actually from Long Island. Ever been?"

"No, but I've heard it's nice."

"Lots of beaches, not too far from the city. I grew up in Brooklyn, but my parents yanked me out of school and moved us to the suburbs when I was a teenager. I hated it at first, but I adjusted."

Justine nodded. "I guess people can adjust to almost anything."

She'd always thought of New Yorkers as snotty know-it-alls, but Jill was different. They had an instant connection.

One by one, the women filed into the recreation room, towels folded under their arms. Justine hadn't expected a big turnout, but to her surprise, the room filled quickly. For a moment, she worried there might not be enough space.

Jill stepped to the front of the room.

"Hi, I'm Jill, your yoga instructor. I'm so glad to see so many of you here today. I don't have yoga mats just yet, but a local fitness club is donating some. For now, towels will do just fine."

She looked around, her voice warm and inviting. "Today, we'll learn a little about the history of yoga, how to breathe properly, and some basic poses. We'll end with meditation."

A few inmates exchanged skeptical glances.

"Yoga originated in India," Jill continued. "It's a practice that combines physical postures, breathing techniques, and meditation. It helps calm the mind, reduce anxiety, and build awareness of the present moment. How many of you are familiar with yoga?"

Only one woman raised her hand.

All eyes turned toward the back of the room. Becky sat cross-legged on her towel in the lotus position, her back straight and eyes half-closed.

"What's your name?" Jill asked.

"Becky."

"Would you be willing to join me up front and assist with the class?"

Becky hesitated. After all the grief she'd gotten from the others, she wasn't sure. But something in Jill's tone made it hard to refuse. She stood and walked quietly to the front.

"This is called the lotus position," Jill said, motioning to Becky. "It helps prepare the mind for meditation. Meditation allows you to disconnect from your physical surroundings and connect with your inner self. It's a powerful tool — not just for healing, but for coping with addiction, stress, and reentry into the outside world."

Jill rang a small brass bell, its delicate chime floating through the room.

"We ring the bell to signal our arrival — to invite divinity, and dispel negative energy."

The women listened, rapt.

"Let's begin with breathing. Sit comfortably. Place your hands together in front of your heart. Close your eyes. Inhale slowly through your nose... exhale through your mouth. Feel your body soften with every breath. Let go of tension. Let go of toxic thoughts."

A gentle rhythm of breath filled the room.

Jill opened her eyes. "Now, I'll show you five foundational poses. These are the building blocks of any yoga practice."

She demonstrated alongside Becky, naming each one as she moved through them:

"Tadasana — Mountain Pose. Uttanasana — Forward Fold. Utthita Chaturanga Dandasana — Plank Pose. Adho Mukha Svanasana — Downward Dog. And finally, Balasana — the Child's Pose."

The women followed as best they could. There was awkward giggling at first, but soon the room grew quiet again. Focused. Still.

Jill rang the bell once more.

"Let's end with meditation. Sit comfortably. If you're uncomfortable closing your eyes, pick a spot on the floor to focus on. Just breathe—naturally. Notice how your body moves with each inhale... and each exhale."

The room held its breath, as if time itself had paused.

"Namaste," Jill said softly. "We bow to the divine within each of you. It's a way of honoring ourselves and each other. Please repeat it with me."

"Namaste," the women echoed.

Jill smiled. "Next time, we'll have mats, and we'll move into the Warrior poses."

As the class ended, the women crowded around Jill and Becky, faces flushed with energy and curiosity.

"I can't believe how good I feel," Stacy said, her eyes wide. "It's like all my frustration just... drained out of me."

"Same," said another. "I haven't felt this calm in years."

Justine stood back for a moment, watching the scene unfold. A yoga class might not fix broken lives or erase trauma—but it had created something new. A stillness.

Library Assignment

Justine was heading to the patio after breakfast when a guard stopped her.

"Morgan! New job assignment. Report to the library. Ask for Michelle."

"The library?" Her mind flashed to Maryann's promise to recommend her for the position if she got released. She headed there immediately.

Inside, a tall, lanky woman in an oversized uniform stood at the counter. Her pants were too short, but she'd cuffed the hems, turning them into makeshift capris.

"I'm Justine. I've been assigned to work here."

"Oh, yes. Maryann's friend." Michelle looked her over. "She said you were smart and honest—though maybe a little naïve. They were gonna give this spot to someone else, but I fought for you."

Justine's smile dimmed at the naïveté remark.

Michelle laughed. "Don't be so sensitive. You need thick skin to work in here. This place is the second busiest in the joint—after the cafeteria."

Justine thought about how much easier it would be to help people with access to books and the computer. "I'm sure I can handle it."

"Great. Let's get started. Oh—and you're also on book cart duty. Every day. Some inmates like to read in their cubes."

"I've seen it come around. It's as popular as mail call."

"You wouldn't think it, but we've got some serious readers in here."

The overhead lights flickered.

"Someone's gettin' the juice," Michelle said.

Justine froze for a beat before remembering Maryann's warning—Michelle was a jokester.

Michelle grinned. "You gotta lighten up, Morgan."

"I guess I'm a little too serious."

"Stick around. That'll change. We've got it good here."

Just then, a side door opened, and a disorderly group of women spilled in.

Michelle groaned. "That's the GED class. What a joke."

"What do you mean?" Justine asked.

"No structure. Some of these women are lifers with no chance at parole. They're just looking to dodge job assignments. They disrupt the ones who actually want to learn."

"Why doesn't the teacher do something?"

"Old man Jefferson? He's scared of his own shadow."

"Then why's he even here?"

"No one else wanted the gig. I think he just likes getting away from his 'wifey-poo' for the day."

"That's terrible. How does anyone learn anything?"

"They don't. But they'll still get a diploma. Makes the prison look good on paper—but it doesn't stop them from coming back once they're out."

"Has anyone tried to recruit someone else?"

"Doubt it. Who's gonna bother?"

Maybe I will, Justine thought.

She was pulled from her thoughts when a sun-weathered woman with a determined look stepped inside.

"Is there a law section in here?" she asked.

"Small one," Michelle replied.

The woman's eyes landed on Justine. "Hey—you're that Justice girl, right?"

"That's what they call me," Justine said with a cautious smile. "I've studied a bit of law and helped a few people. Still learning, though."

"Maybe you can help me. I'm Darcy. Trying to get clemency. Could use your expertise."

"What are you in for?"

"They say I poisoned my husband. But I'm innocent."

"What evidence did they use?"

"That's the thing—they didn't have any at first. The original autopsy said no arsenic. Then the prosecution brought in their own expert, and *suddenly* it was a match."

"This is my first day in the library," Justine said. "But give me some time—I'll research it on the computer."

"Where are you from?"

"Montana."

"Bet it's cold there."

"Colder than a witch's tit."

Darcy laughed. "What's your name? I'll give you my case number later."

"Justine Morgan."

That evening, after her shift ended, Justine went to see the warden.

"I don't oversee the GED program," Mr. Atwood said. "You'll need to contact the Bureau of Prisons." He opened a drawer, rummaged around, and handed her a bulky directory. "Here. Knock yourself out."

"Thanks," Justine said, leaving with the book—and a smile. The warden liked her. That made two people in her corner: Atwood and Jenkins, the guard.

Back in her cell, she stretched out on her bunk and drafted the letter:

To Whom It May Concern,

I'm writing regarding the GED program at Larsen Correctional Institution. The system isn't working as efficiently as it could. While many inmates attend in hopes of earning their diplomas, others are there to avoid work details and end up disrupting the class for those who want to learn.

I propose a two-track system. One for inmates up for parole or release within the next two to five years, and another for lifers and long-term inmates, integrating vocational programs like culinary arts, music, or visual arts. Splitting the class would allow both groups to benefit from customized instruction geared toward their goals.

It costs approximately $20,000 a year to incarcerate one inmate. Only a fraction of that is invested in education or skill development. Multiply that by the number of inmates in Florida, and the cost becomes staggering. We must do better.

Please consider restructuring the current system. It would benefit the inmates, the prison, and society as a whole.

Sincerely,
Justine Morgan

GED

It was visitation day, and most inmates were busy hugging loved ones, catching up on missed birthdays, and wiping away tears. Justine took the rare quiet as a chance to dig into Darcy's case.

She typed *Darcy Mayfield* into the search bar, and a slurry of news articles filled the screen. Her eyes froze on the first headline.

"Florida Woman Poisons Husband."

She clicked. The article loaded slowly, as if reluctant to share the truth.

A Florida woman was convicted of killing her police officer husband with arsenic-laced supplements. Initial blood tests showed no signs of poison, but a second test — ordered by the prosecution — came back positive for a toxic substance. Arsenic levels were inconclusive. The medical examiner called the discrepancy 'odd' but offered no further explanation. The victim, Officer Paul Mayfield, had worked with the local police department for over twenty years and had many friends in both the precinct and the courts.

Justine stared at the screen. *He was a cop,* she thought. *She never stood a chance.* Darcy had been railroaded. Framed, even. Justine felt certain there was enough to build an argument for clemency—maybe even an appeal.

She couldn't wait to tell Darcy what she'd found. But since that first conversation, she hadn't seen her. After asking around, she learned Darcy was on the graveyard shift in the infirmary.

"She used to be a nurse," one redhead told her, puffing on a hand-rolled cigarette under the awning. "But don't expect Florence Nightingale. Now she changes bedpans."

"Have you seen her today?"

"She was out here this morning. Then poof—med unit."

Justine hatched a plan.

She approached the new female guard, holding her stomach. "Excuse me. I'm getting sharp pains in my abdomen. I feel like I'm gonna pass out."

The guard didn't blink. "Probably something you ate. Go back to your cube and puke it up. You'll feel better."

"No, this isn't food poisoning. It's been going on for a week. I think it's my appendix."

The guard narrowed her eyes. "Don't try playing games with me. I've seen every trick."

Justine gave up and headed back to her cube—but before she could get there, she was summoned to the warden's office.

She knocked. "Mr. Atwood?"

"Come in. Close the door."

"Is something wrong?"

"I'd say so." His voice was clipped. "You wrote to the Bureau of Prisons about the GED program."

Justine paled. "I—I just wanted to improve it."

"Well, now there is no program. They're investigating. Classes are suspended until further notice."

"I didn't mean—"

"It's not just on you," he said, sighing. "I gave you that directory. Should've known better."

"Is there anything I can do to fix this?"

"No," he said flatly. "You've done enough. We'll wait for BOP to finish their review."

*****

Word spread through the prison. Justine was the reason the class was canceled. She had killed the GED program. Whispers followed her everywhere.

"You'd better watch your back," Sara warned. "I heard Sharkesha in Level Four wants to make an example out of you. Said you're messing with the system."

Justine went to the only guard she trusted.

"I think I made things worse," she admitted to CO Jenkins. "I tried to help, but I've ended up making enemies. And now no one's learning anything."

He nodded, his expression calm. "What you're doing is admirable. But you're going about it the wrong way."

"I just want to give these women a shot—something to help them on the outside."

Jenkins scratched his chin. "My wife teaches at the state college. I'll ask if she or her colleagues can volunteer. Maybe bring some fresh energy into this place."

"You'd do that?"

"I'll try. In the meantime, lay low."

*****

Darcy finally rotated back to the afternoon shift and came into the library.

Justine jumped up. "You're back!"

"Only for a shift," Darcy said. "I'm not scrubbing toilets today."

"I have something for you." Justine pulled out a manila envelope. "I looked into your case. The autopsy reports were contradictory. You have a real chance. This is the clemency application. No fee. Just sign it and send it with your court papers."

Darcy smiled. "You're serious?"

"I already printed everything you'll need."

"You're amazing. I didn't think anyone cared."

"I care," Justine said softly.

On the way back to her pod, Justine stopped at the laundry room. She didn't expect anyone to be there.

But two women stood near the machines. One swung a sock like a lasso, weighted with something heavy.

Her gut tightened. *Trouble.*

Then she saw her. Sharkesha.

"Well, if it ain't little Miss Justice," Sharkesha sneered.

Justine turned to leave, but the woman lunged. One grabbed her arm. The other shoved her against the dryer. Sharkesha stepped in, eyes gleaming.

"You really thought you could mess with the program and walk away?"

Justine braced herself.

Whack. Whack. Whack.

She opened her eyes — only to find Sharkesha and her friend on the floor. CO Jenkins stood above them, baton raised.

"Told you to lay low," he muttered.

Justine let out a shaky breath. "You have no idea how glad I am to see you."

He offered a half-smile. "Let's get you cleaned up, Justice Girl."

*****

A month later, Justine was shelving books in the library when she heard screams of joy echoing down the hallway.

"Justine, we did it!" Darcy burst in, eyes wide with excitement. "My application's been forwarded to the Office of Clemency Investigations. I have a hearing next week!"

"That's amazing! Will you need to be there?"

"No, but I'm not leaving anything to chance. I asked the warden for permission to appear by video, and he approved it."

Justine hugged her. "I'm so proud of you."

The hearing went well. One week later, the news came: **Darcy had been granted clemency.** Her release was scheduled for the next day.

Justine organized a small going-away party. In the commons, a cluster of women from Darcy's pod gathered around her, laughing, sharing snacks, and hugging goodbye. Justine stood off to the side with Peaches and Stella, her own cellmates flanking her.

"What's all the hoopla about?" Stella asked, eyeing the crowd.

"Darcy's getting out," Justine said, smiling. "The governor granted her clemency."

Stella raised a brow. "You don't really believe she's innocent, do you?"

"The autopsy report was tainted," Justine said. "The trial records showed the arsenic test was inconclusive."

"That's because she didn't use arsenic," Peaches said, folding her arms.

Justine frowned. "What do you mean?"

"I heard she used Visine. Told another girl in her pod all about it. She laced her husband's coffee."

"Visine? You mean the eye drops?"

"Yeah. Tetrahydrozoline," Peaches said. "Ingested in large doses, it can cause seizures, coma, even death. But if the coroner wasn't looking for it, they'd never find it."

Justine stared at her. "But... why would she do that? Was it self-defense?"

"Nope. Money. Her husband had a half-million-dollar life insurance policy. She wanted to collect."

"But if she was convicted of murder, wouldn't that void the payout?"

"Exactly. That's why she needed clemency. Word is, the insurance company pulled strings behind the scenes. They weren't about to pay out unless the conviction was cleared."

Justine's mouth went dry. "We have to tell someone. The governor—there's still time."

Amy walked by and snorted. "Too late. She's being released tomorrow morning. Paperwork's already signed."

Justine's hands dropped to her sides.

She thought back to her first week inside, to something the warden had said with a weary shrug. "Every inmate claims they're innocent."

She hadn't wanted to believe it. But now... lesson learned.

Appeal Denied

Pushing the book cart from pod to pod, Justine found herself learning more than she ever expected. The Latina pod buzzed with energy. Music played from a smuggled speaker, and women danced the salsa and macarena like they were at a block party instead of behind bars.

But amid the celebration, one woman stood out — thin, with nervous eyes and a permanent crease of worry etched across her brow.

Justine leaned over to Stephanie. "What's her story?"

"That's Martina," Stephanie said. "New fish. In for kidnapping."

"Kidnapping?" Justine asked. "What'd she do — snatch someone's baby?"

"No. Her own kids."

"What?"

"She was married to a bastard who beat her and the kids. Real sicko. She got help from a women's shelter and filed for divorce. Brought the judge evidence—photos, hospital records, you name it. But he still gave the guy joint custody. Said the kids needed a father." Stephanie rolled her eyes. "The court gave him weekends and one month every summer."

Justine frowned. "Didn't anyone check on the kids?"

"They came back crying. Sometimes with bruises. Her daughter finally told her he was touching her. So, Martina grabbed the kids and ran. Almost made it to the Keys. Cops flagged her car and dragged her back."

"That's... horrific. Where are the kids now?"

"He took them to Cuba. She can't reach them from inside, and nobody's helping."

Justine felt a knot form in her chest. "I can't believe the court gave him custody."

Stephanie shrugged. "He's their father. The system won't step in unless someone dies."

"There are good foster families out there. Kids deserve to feel safe."

Stephanie's gaze turned cold. "You think foster care is some kind of fairytale?"

Justine hesitated. "I didn't mean—"

"I was in foster care. My mom got popped for crack, and they split me and my sister up. She got lucky. I didn't. The couple that took me in wanted the check, not a kid." She exhaled sharply. "Justice is blind—and it likes it that way."

Justine swallowed hard. "I'm sorry."

She pushed the cart into the segregated pod—the Psych Ward. The women here weren't assigned jobs. Most sat blank-faced, staring at the TV or coloring on placemats, drugged into stillness. Drool slipped down one woman's chin as she rocked slowly in her chair.

Rumor was that the staff kept the meds strong to avoid dealing with outbursts. But as the drugs wore off, agitation kicked in. One woman near the wall waved her arms, trying to get Justine's attention. Justine moved closer, but another woman grabbed her wrist.

"They're trying to kill me," she whispered, wild-eyed. Her age was impossible to guess—her face deeply lined, but her voice small and scared.

Justine gently pulled away and turned back to the woman who'd been waving—only to see her suddenly slam her forehead against the metal table. Again. And again. Blood streamed down her face.

Guards rushed in, restrained her, and hauled her off.

"What happens to her now?" Justine asked one of them, shaken.

"She'll be sedated, stripped, and put in a paper gown. Observation cell. Probably just needs her dosage tweaked."

Justine stared at the smeared blood. Maybe the Psych Ward wasn't as "easy" as it looked.

She moved on to level four—*seg*, the pod reserved for the most volatile inmates. The air felt thicker here. Cells had solid metal doors. Though they were allowed out during the day, nights were spent in lockdown.

Only a few women sat near the television on the second tier. The pod was eerily quiet.

"Where is everyone?" she asked the guard on duty.

"Anger management class," he said with a smirk. "New program the warden approved."

Justine smiled. *Finally*, some of her pestering was paying off.

On her way out, she passed a cell where two women were making out. She looked away, but not fast enough. One of them noticed and gave her a slow, mocking smile, licking her lips.

Justine kept walking.

There were rules against sexual misconduct — zero tolerance, officially. But everyone knew it wasn't enforced. She'd once asked Amy about it.

Amy had just laughed. "Everyone needs love, Justine."

*****

Two months had passed since Justine had last heard from Blake Sullivan. Just when she was beginning to lose hope of ever getting out, Officer Jenkins showed up at her pod.

"You've got a visitor."

Her heart leapt. *This is it*, she thought, practically running to the front building. But as soon as she entered the visitation room, her hope deflated like a punctured balloon.

Blake's face said it all.

"I'm sorry, Justine. Your appeal was denied."

She sank into the chair. "Why?"

"The judge upheld the mandatory sentencing statute. He applied the law as it's written."

"But I had a crappy lawyer," she said, bitterness rising in her throat.

Blake leaned in. "Did you take a polygraph?"

"Yes. I passed."

"Why didn't your attorney present the results at trial?"

"I don't know. He was brand new — maybe his second case. The public defender assigned him. I didn't know I had a choice."

"That's it then," Blake said. "I think we have grounds for a Writ of Habeas Corpus."

Justine's brow furrowed. "How's that different from an appeal?"

"An appeal corrects legal errors. A habeas corpus petition challenges the legality of your imprisonment itself. In your case, we'd argue ineffective assistance of counsel. But first, I'll file a motion asking a panel of appellate judges to review evidence that wasn't presented at trial."

"Would there be another jury?"

"No. The appellate court doesn't retry cases. It reviews the trial court's record for fairness and constitutional violations. I'll write a legal brief laying out the argument."

Justine exhaled slowly. "Can I ask you something?"

"Sure. Shoot."

"What made you become a lawyer?"

He paused, then said, "Social justice. I've always believed access to opportunity shouldn't depend on your zip code or your bank account. I wanted to challenge the system, make it fairer."

"Isn't that what checks and balances are for?"

"In theory. But justice doesn't always play out evenly. Poverty, race, and social status often tip the scales."

"And gender," Justine added. "Women experience the system differently. It rarely accounts for the complexity of our situations—abuse, trauma, mental health. They lump everyone together without context."

He nodded. "True. And for a long time, women's issues were sidelined. When I graduated from law school, most of the guys were focused on corporate law. Women's rights didn't even make the conversation."

Justine leaned forward. "And then there's codependency. The whole Patty Hearst syndrome—when people make bad decisions because they're trapped emotionally or psychologically. I wonder if it could ever be used as a legitimate defense."

Blake smiled thoughtfully. "It would be a hard argument to win—but it's not crazy. The system's slow to accept nuance, but it's not impossible."

She found herself smiling back, surprised at how easy he was to talk to—how much common ground they shared. She could've sat there all day.

A guard tapped the glass. "Five more minutes."

Blake rose and adjusted his coat. "We're going to be spending a lot of time together over the next few months."

Justine blushed. "I'm looking forward to it."

He grinned. "Since you're working in the library now, study up on habeas corpus. Even if things don't go our way, you'll walk away with an education."

"I will," she said. "Promise."

Spring Renewal

Religion came to life in the spring. Easter brought out the faithful—even in prison. Attendance at church services swelled with inmates seeking redemption or, at the very least, distraction. Justine, however, had little tolerance for the loud proclamations of those who claimed to have a direct line to God. She was especially wary of the ones who insisted on praying for her.

Thankfully, her cellmates weren't among them. Gail's faith was steady but private; she'd had enough of Bible-thumpers. Laura openly declared herself an atheist, and Doris was even more blunt—" God turned his back on me when I was eleven," she said, "the day my brother raped me."

Justine's spirituality was more of a quiet stirring than a booming voice from above. She remembered childhood Easters—how her family celebrated with a patchwork of traditions. Alongside the Easter lamb, there was always matzah ball soup—a mix of Jewish and pagan rituals. Her father would recount the ten plagues while her mother reminded her that Jesus died for her sins. The best part, though, was always the basket — cellophane-wrapped and filled with buttered matzos and a hollow chocolate bunny. She'd stare at it, trying to decide whether to eat the ears or the candy eyes first.

There were no chocolate rabbits in prison, but the inmates made do. A local farm had donated hams past their sell-by dates and sacks of potatoes going soft. The kitchen boiled the potatoes and mashed them with gobs of butter. For dessert, they served vanilla cupcakes topped with green-dyed coconut "grass" and cheesecake made from vanilla pudding and squishy cheese pressed over crushed graham crackers.

Vicky and Beth, two cafeteria workers, were more interested in the leftovers than the celebration itself.

Vicky eyed the pile of discarded potato skins. "Hey, we can make prison hooch with these."

Beth grinned. "Yeah? And where are we hiding it this time?"

Vicky looked up. "See those fiberglass tiles? They're not fixed in place. Same as the ones in the library."

Beth nodded, impressed. "You're a genius."

*****

A few days after Easter dinner, when the sugar buzz from coconut-topped cupcakes had worn off, and the potato hooch was safely hidden above the ceiling tiles, a sudden announcement crackled over the PA system.

"All inmates report to the chapel immediately."

Justine froze mid-shelving in the library. She glanced at CO Jenkins, who was stationed by the door.

"What's going on?"

He shrugged, but there was a twinkle in his eye. "Rumor has it, the education program's getting a makeover. Word is, your letter to the Board of Prisons ruffled some feathers. I heard the ACLU's been sniffing around."

Justine's pulse quickened. She rushed to the chapel, where the pews filled quickly with murmuring inmates. At the podium stood a petite woman in a crisp beige dress, her manicured toes peeking through stylish peep-toe heels. Everything about her screamed government efficiency with a side of spa weekends.

"Hello, ladies," the woman began, her voice poised. "I'm Ms. Davis. It's come to our attention that the educational offerings at this facility have fallen short. Effective immediately, the GED program will be completely restructured to better serve both inmates and staff."

Justine sat up straighter.

"We believe that the collective pursuit of learning is a human right," Ms. Davis continued. "That's why we're implementing a new curriculum—one built on structure, opportunity, and rehabilitation."

She smiled as murmurs spread through the room. "There will now be three education levels, allowing for smaller class sizes and more tailored instruction. Each level will cover reading, math, science, social studies, and language arts. Students will be assessed through placement tests, and those who complete a level will be invited to mentor others — creating a peer-led model of growth and success."

Hands shot up. A woman in the third row didn't wait to be called. "What if we're in the SHU? Can we still take the test?"

"Those in solitary confinement won't be eligible for exams," Ms. Davis explained, "but they will be provided with learning materials. Upon reentry into the general population, they may rejoin the program through a good behavior points system."

Another voice called out. "What about lifers?"

"Lifers with the possibility of parole may be admitted on a case-by-case basis, pending a letter of recommendation from a caseworker and a clean disciplinary record. For inmates without parole, we'll offer programs in creative writing, visual arts, and self-development."

A sharp voice cut through the crowd. "So, what? Basket weaving?"

Laughter rippled through the room. Tension crackled. Ms. Davis looked momentarily flustered.

"No," she said, raising her voice over the growing chatter. "Our vision is to build a fully operational educational and vocational community within these walls. Vocational classes will include nursing assistance, clerical training, and culinary arts."

"You mean cheap prison labor," Doris muttered from the back.

Ms. Davis didn't flinch. "These will be competitive roles. You'll apply just like on the outside. But unlike standard prison detail, these positions will pay double."

By the end of the meeting, the room had shifted. Frustration turned to curiosity. Then to cautious optimism. The blame that had once been heaped on Justine for disrupting the GED program melted away. Now, inmates approached her with nods of respect.

She hadn't just shaken the system. She'd stirred it into motion.

*****

Amy's release came a few days later. Justine was sad to see her go, but proud to watch her walk free, chin high and future open. Like clockwork, a new wave of inmates marched in behind her. Some looked like deer caught in headlights — nervous, wide-eyed, uncertain. Others wore hardened expressions, already calculating their place in the hierarchy.

Among them were women with serious charges, even violent ones — but many had earned the right to transfer from higher-security units. In an effort to reward model behavior, the prison offered an incentive: four days shaved off a sentence for every month of good conduct. It wasn't freedom — but it was a glimmer of it.

And now, with real educational and vocational paths in place, Justine knew — sooner or later — more women would leave through the front gate, not in chains.

*****

Amy's bunk didn't stay empty for long. The new girl, Laura, was barely nineteen but carried herself with the world-weariness of someone twice her age. It didn't take long for Justine to realize the girl had issues — serious ones.

Much like Camila, Justine's former cellmate, Laura, made every effort to look seductive in the drab prison uniform, leaving the top unbuttoned just enough to show cleavage. Her hair was styled in a sharp bob that reminded Justine of the Dutch Boy paint can label — sleek, blunt, and oddly defiant.

Confidence wasn't something Laura lacked. From the moment she arrived, she set her sights on the correction officers, working her charm to gain special treatment. Justine spotted her more than once sneaking into the supply room when no one was supposed to be there. Everyone knew the rules: staff and inmates were never to mingle beyond professional interaction. But as Justine had learned, some rules were only enforced when it was convenient.

Even the female officers turned a blind eye, unwilling to cross their fellow COs. But the inmates noticed. They grumbled about the extra privileges Laura received — getting to meals first, skipping shower lines, and dodging the chores the rest were assigned.

It wasn't long before Laura latched onto Allen Murphy, a middle-aged guard known for his wandering eyes and stale-cigarette smell. With slick black hair and icy blue eyes, Murphy was handsome enough—if you could overlook the cough that preceded his arrival like a warning bell. His reputation was no secret; Justine had often felt his gaze trailing her like smoke. But now, with Laura in his sights, Justine could finally breathe easier.

Despite her antics, Justine found herself liking Laura. She was sharp, funny, and easy to talk to. Late at night, when the lights dimmed and the hum of prison life softened, the two women whispered across the narrow space between their bunks.

"Why do you flirt with the COs?" Justine asked one night.

Laura sighed. "Because I need to feel loved."

"Not me," Justine said. "If I could wish for anything, it wouldn't be love. It'd be contentment."

"Contentment? That's boring."

"No. If I were content, I wouldn't keep chasing things that don't exist."

Laura chuckled. "Well, you're not going to find that here. But I can find love—or at least a distraction."

Justine didn't answer. Instead, her thoughts drifted to darker questions—like what would happen if Laura got pregnant. As far as she knew, no one had become pregnant while serving time, but new arrivals sometimes came in showing signs of pregnancy.

She remembered one inmate clearly—a twenty-five-year-old Cuban woman convicted of shoplifting. She'd had no idea she was pregnant when she was sentenced to five years. Within months, her belly had swollen, and when the time came, she begged Justine to go with her as the officer wheeled her toward the infirmary.

Justine had never forgotten the moment the CO handcuffed the woman's arm to the wheelchair mid-contraction.

"Is that really necessary?" she asked him.

"It's procedure."

"It's inhumane," Justine shot back.

Inside the medical unit, the CO transferred the handcuffs from the chair to the woman's wrists. Moments later, the doctor stormed in.

"Why is this woman restrained?" he demanded.

"Policy," the officer said. "They're inmates—even in labor."

"Not in my operating room. Remove the cuffs. I'll take full responsibility."

The CO hesitated.

"Oh, come on," the doctor snapped. "You think she's going to jump off the table and make a run for it—with a baby halfway out of her?"

The cuffs were removed. But the moment had etched itself into Justine's memory—a stark reminder of how dignity was the first thing to disappear behind bars.

Crack

Justine took extra care getting ready to meet with her lawyer. She even wore the small tin of makeup Camila had left behind as a parting gift when she was released. A touch of color, she thought, might lift her spirits — or at least give her confidence.

Whenever Blake came to visit, they were granted a small private room in the administration building, far from the clamor of the general visitation area. As he pulled his chair close and spread legal briefs between them, Justine could feel his breath on her cheek. When their knees accidentally brushed, her whole body tensed with longing. She missed the intimacy of human connection — the simple comfort of a man's touch.

"Are you married?" she asked softly.

"No," Blake replied. "But I'd like to be someday. I want a big family. A bunch of kids."

Justine laughed, surprised. "Really? You don't seem the type."

"Oh?" he grinned. "What type do I seem?"

"A workaholic," she teased.

"You're not wrong," he admitted. "I'm passionate about standing up for minorities and fighting injustice. But I think I could have both—purpose and family."

She smiled. His openness made her feel safe. "What do you do when you're not saving the world?"

"My parents left me a small horse stable," he said. "When I can, I drive upstate and take a horse out. Helps me clear my head."

"Wow. How many horses do you have?"

"Five. Two of them are old—they were my parents' favorites. I couldn't bring myself to sell them or put them to pasture."

"Must be a lot of work."

"I've got help. A woman from the neighboring farm takes care of the barn. But I try to go whenever I can. My dad put me on a horse when I was three. I could ride before I could even run."

Time melted away, and before Justine knew it, the guard was tapping on the window with his baton.

"Time's up."

Justine sighed. "I wish you could stay longer."

"I'll find a reason to come back before the end of the month," Blake promised. "Want me to bring you anything?"

"Coffee," she said without hesitation. "The stuff they serve here tastes like dishwater."

He chuckled. "I doubt they'll let me bring in a thermos, but I could smuggle in some instant. Starbucks makes a decent one."

"That would be heaven," she whispered.

She wanted to hug him, to hold on just a moment longer. But the guard entered before she could move. She kept her eyes down, hiding the emotions she couldn't suppress, ashamed for him to see her this way. She didn't even glance back as she was led away, though her heart ached to.

Outside, the sky was gray and thick with smoke.

"Something's on fire," the guard said, pointing toward the rising plumes.

"It's coming from the library!" Justine shouted. She pulled toward the building instinctively. "We have to save the books!"

"Stop!" the guard barked, yanking her cuffs. "You're out of bounds, inmate."

"But—"

"No buts. Let it go."

Inside the main building, he removed her cuffs and handed her off to another guard with strict orders: "Keep her away from the library."

Justine turned to Officer Jenkins as soon as she spotted him. "Please," she begged. "Can you find out what happened?"

He looked conflicted. "Justine, I can't keep doing this. Staff is getting suspicious, and the inmates are starting to talk."

"I know, but just this once. I won't ask again."

He sighed. "All right. But this is the last time."

She spent lunch in the cafeteria, barely touching her food, stomach too knotted with worry. Rumors flew around the room, but no one knew anything for sure.

After the meal, she rushed back to her pod. Jenkins was there—but cold, unreadable. She approached him anyway.

"Did you find out what caused the fire?"

"Two inmates were smoking crack behind the bookshelves. With some prison hooch, no less."

Her heart sank. "Do you know who?"

"I can't give you that information, inmate." The word stung more than usual.

"Were the books saved?"

"The library's officially closed. That's all I can say."

Justine eventually found Michelle, who filled in the rest. Most of the books were ruined — soaked by the fire sprinklers. The computers were saved, but they had been relocated to the warden's office. For now, the library was off-limits. And Justine was out of a job.

Worse yet, the GED program was suspended again. The entire prison went into lockdown. The two girls responsible were sent to solitary confinement, but that didn't stop the guards from tearing apart every cube in a full sweep.

"I knew it," Gail muttered darkly. "You can always tell who's on crack by their teeth. They hide their lips when they talk and never smile."

Justine sat silently, staring at her now-useless library badge. So much progress — undone by smoke and ash.

College Courses

Justine was lying in bed when Laura burst into the cell and shook her shoulder.

"Get up! There's someone here from the college. His name's Paul Peterson. He's heading the new education initiative. He's speaking in the common room right now."

Justine jolted upright, heart racing. After months of writing letters and pushing for college programs, it was finally happening.

She slipped into her uniform, ignoring the growl in her stomach. Breakfast could wait. *I have to get into that program.*

When she entered the common room, it was already buzzing with energy. Inmates filled the rows of plastic chairs, many sitting straighter than usual, their eyes locked on the speaker at the podium — a trim man in khakis and a sports coat, with the confident posture of someone used to being listened to.

Justine grabbed a seat in the front row.

"A few religious colleges offer correspondence courses for prisoners," Mr. Peterson explained. "There is a catch: you may study any subject, but you must complete at least one religious course as part of the curriculum. Now, here are the requirements:

One—you must have a high school diploma or GED.

Two—you need a letter of recommendation from your case manager.

Three—you must be discipline-free for ninety days prior to enrollment."

Justine sat up straighter. *This is it. This is my chance.*

She waited until the crowd dispersed, then approached Mr. Peterson directly.

"Mr. Peterson," she said. "I'm very interested in the program. I've been waiting a long time for an opportunity like this."

He looked at her kindly. "What field are you interested in?"

"Law," she said, voice unsteady with emotion. She tried not to sound desperate—but she *was* desperate.

"That's a lofty goal," he said. "What's your educational background?"

"I have a bachelor's in criminal justice from the University of Miami. I was working on my master's when I was arrested. I want to go to law school."

Peterson's brows lifted slightly. "You do realize you won't be able to sit for the Bar, even if you finish law school."

"My lawyer is working on that," she said. "He's filing a Writ of Habeas Corpus."

"Still," Peterson said carefully, "even with a successful appeal, most states don't allow convicted felons to take the Bar. Even with a pardon, you'd need an expungement. And even then, disclosure of your full criminal and mental health history would likely be required."

"There has to be a way," Justine said, firmer now. "I've read stories about former inmates who fought for a second chance—and won."

He nodded slowly. "Look. I can't promise anything. But I'll see what I can do to get you into an online law program."

That afternoon, Justine made an appointment with her case manager, Arthur Labella. He was a soft-spoken man in his late forties with salt-and-pepper hair and tired eyes.

"Mr. Labella, I'd like to apply for an online law degree. I need a letter of recommendation."

He thumbed through her file and glanced up. "I admire your determination. Looks like you got a raw deal. I'll write you a glowing letter."

"Thank you," she said, eyes burning.

Peterson stayed true to his word. Within two weeks, she was accepted into a correspondence program through St. Thomas University School of Law in Miami. Two other colleges had also approved her application, but St. Thomas had ties to the Center for Legal Studies—a vital link in her legal journey.

Her courses would include DVDs, textbooks, study guides, and limited access to the one computer donated for the program. She would also need permission to use a DVD player for her lectures.

The cost was steep. She had a trust fund, but her father controlled it. She could only hope he'd finally let go of the reins.

That morning, she skipped breakfast and stood impatiently in the phone line, rehearsing what she would say. When the call connected, it went to voicemail.

"Hi, Mom," she said, her voice trembling with excitement. "I have incredible news. I've been accepted into law school. It's real, Mom. I'm going to be a lawyer. Call me when you get this. Please."

She hung up and wiped her eyes, her heart thudding with equal parts fear and hope. This wasn't just about proving her innocence anymore. It was about rewriting her future.

*****

Karen, a thin, brown-haired woman with deep shadows under her eyes, sat beside Justine in the food hall. Her face wasn't conventionally pretty, but when she smiled, her wide mouth lit up her whole expression. She had been inside for 26 years.

"Do you like to read?" she asked, stirring her instant coffee. "I just finished a great book — a love story set in Italy. *Light of the Moon*. I swear, I forgot I was in prison while reading it. I felt sad when it ended."

"Thanks," Justine replied, "but my eyes are really bad. I get a pounding headache every time I try to read."

Justine perked up. "I might have something that can help. It's a plastic magnifier sheet. You lay it over the page, and it makes the words bigger. I used it for reading at night under my flashlight, but I don't really need it anymore. Come by my cube later — I'll give it to you."

Justine didn't expect her to show up, but later that afternoon, Karen appeared outside her cube, hesitant but hopeful.

"I used to read all the time," she said, taking the sheet in her hands. "I was an A-student before I went off the rails and got swept up in... well, you know. Bad choices. Worse people."

"You should join the GED class," Justine offered gently. "You might really enjoy it. I'm not sure where they're holding it now since the fire closed the library, but I'm sure they'll find a spot."

Karen looked away. "What's the use? I'm never getting out of here."

Justine heard the hollow ache in her voice and didn't try to argue with facts or false hope. Instead, she leaned closer.

"You don't know that for sure. Even if the outside world seems out of reach, sometimes it finds its way to you. Change can happen, even here."

Karen nodded slowly, clutching the magnifier.

"I'll think about it," she said, and for the first time, her smile wasn't forced.

Justine watched her go, her own heart heavy. She understood those feelings too well — what it meant to live without hope, and how powerful even the smallest flicker could be.

*****

GED classes had been moved to the chapel, but there weren't enough textbooks to go around. Justine thought back to an article she had once read about the Prison Library Project — a nonprofit in Claremont, California that provided books and educational materials to incarcerated people across the country.

Determined to act, she made her way to the warden's office. The door was already ajar, so she knocked lightly and peeked in.

Mr. Atwood glanced up from his desk. "What now, Justine?" he said, half-smiling, not the least bit surprised to see her.

She stepped inside. "The head of the education initiative, Mr. Peterson, said he'd write me a recommendation for law school. I might need help from time to time — someone to talk through legal concepts and case studies. Would you be willing to discuss some of the material with me?"

He set down his pen. "I'm honored you think so highly of me."

"I do. You're the most knowledgeable person I know here. It would mean a lot."

"All right," he said with a nod. "Could be interesting to debate some of the finer points. Yes, Justine, I'll help you."

She smiled. "Thank you. I knew I could count on you."

"One more thing," she added. "Can I use the computer? I want to contact the Prison Library Project to see if they'll donate books to replace what we lost in the fire."

Atwood leaned back in his chair. "I was wondering when you'd ask. You can have half an hour—no more."

"That's all I need."

He chuckled. "Sometimes, I think you're more trouble than you're worth."

"You're a good man, Mr. Atwood."

"If you let that get around, I'll have to throw you in the hole," he said with a wink. Then he stood and grabbed his coffee mug. "Since the library's out of commission, I'm reassigning you to assist with the GED classes. Report to the chapel on Monday. The new teacher's name is Robin Sullivan."

"I'll be glad to help in any way I can."

"Good. I'm going to grab lunch. When I get back, you're done."

Justine was surprised he'd left her alone at the computer. His trust meant something—it lifted her spirits. But she knew prison could turn on a dime. Officer Jenkins had taught her that. After the library fire, he'd abruptly quit. Maybe it was the crack-smoking inmates that broke him. Maybe he got reprimanded for being too lenient. Either way, he was gone.

No Justice

Justine reported to the chapel-turned-classroom on Monday morning. A portable chalkboard stood at the front with "Ms. Sullivan" scrawled across it in bright yellow chalk. The new GED teacher stood nearby — petite, with curly blond hair and thick-rimmed glasses that kept slipping down her nose.

"Hi, I'm Justine," she said. "The warden assigned me to assist with the class."

"Oh, perfect," Ms. Sullivan replied. "I used to teach special ed, so I'm used to challenges. Still, this is my first time working with inmates. I'll admit — I'm a little nervous."

"They can get rowdy," Justine said with a half-smile, "but most just want a chance. You'll be fine."

The door opened, and students began to trickle in. Justine was surprised to see eleven show up. Before the recent changes, they could barely get two or three. What really warmed her heart was spotting Karen among them. She hadn't been sure the woman would come, but there she was—quietly slipping into a seat at the back.

The last to arrive was Doris, Justine's no-nonsense cellmate from Brooklyn.

"Justine," Ms. Sullivan called, "could you please lock the door? We're not allowing late arrivals to disrupt the lesson."

"Yes, ma'am."

Ms. Sullivan passed out notebooks and pens. "Your first assignment," she said, "is to write a short paragraph about what life in prison feels like for you. Be honest. There are no wrong answers."

Silence fell as pens scratched across paper. When the last head lifted, Ms. Sullivan looked around. "Would anyone like to share?"

To Justine's surprise, Karen raised her hand. She stood with shaky hands, clutching her notebook like a lifeline.

"Day after day, I walk these hallways with no privacy," she began, her voice soft but clear. "I'm under surveillance twenty-four hours a day. The only time I'm unreachable is when I'm asleep. Once I move past the regret and stop replaying my bad decisions, I drift into dreams—dreams of home and loved ones—only to be rudely jolted awake by the morning buzzer and the voice announcing, 'Five minutes to count.' I open my eyes to concrete, steel bars, and the blank stares of people who don't care if I live or die. I used to think reading was pointless, but now it opens prison doors in my mind. It's my new escape."

A hush settled over the room. A few women wiped away tears. Even Doris looked moved.

More hands went up. One by one, the women read their pieces — stories of trauma, pain, and unexpected hope. Doris shared something Justine had never heard before. She spoke about growing up in the Brooklyn projects, going to bed hungry, and the silent shame of being molested by her older brother. There were no interruptions, no mocking. Only nods of solidarity. For the first time, the classroom felt like sacred ground.

After the class ended, Karen approached Justine near the podium.

"I loved the book you gave me," she said, eyes shining. "I couldn't put it down."

"I'm so glad," Justine replied.

Karen hesitated, then added, "I've decided to write my own book. I want to tell my story, and I hope you'll help me. It's something I can do with all the time I've got left."

"That's amazing, Karen. I'd be honored to help."

As Karen walked away, Justine stood for a moment in the quiet classroom, letting it all sink in. She'd made a difference in one life. Maybe more. And she knew — deep down — that education wasn't just a path to knowledge. It was the first step toward freedom.

*****

Justine returned to her cube after lunch and stared at the stack of textbooks on her bunk. Homework had become a fixture of her routine — something to anchor her, to keep the flicker of hope alive. She picked up a pen and had barely started on her assignment when the PA system crackled overhead.

"Morgan, report to the visitation room."

Laura poked her head around the curtain. "You've got a visitor."

Justine's heart jumped. Her palms were slick by the time she turned the corridor and stepped into the visitation room — then froze.

Her father was waiting.

He stood stiffly near the table, thinner than she remembered. There was something fragile in the way he held himself, as though seeing her in prison blues had drained the air from his lungs.

She swallowed hard and forced a smile, though her lips trembled.

They sat. For a long moment, neither spoke.

"Where's Mom?" she asked softly.

"She wasn't up to the trip," he said, eyes shifting away.

"Is she okay? I've been calling. No answer. That's not like her."

He hesitated. "She's in the hospital."

Justine's breath caught. "What happened?"

"I found her on the kitchen floor last week. They're still running tests."

"Was it her heart again?"

"No," he said quickly. "They're not sure yet. She's stable. Resting."

Justine pressed her hands to her face. "It's my fault. I've put her through too much."

"Stop that." He reached across the table, taking her hand. "She's strong. She's saving her energy for a Mother's Day visit."

Justine nodded, too choked up to answer. In the background, a TV muttered nonsense to no one.

"How are you holding up?" he asked.

"It's... manageable," she said. "I'm applying to a correspondence law program. But I'll need money for tuition." She hesitated. "I was hoping—"

"Oh, sweetheart." He gave her hand a reassuring squeeze. "Of Course. That money was always meant for your education."

Relief broke across her face. She nearly stood to hug him, but the CO's watchful eye froze her in place. She sat back down, flushed.

"There's just one issue," she added. "I won't be able to sit for the Bar unless the charges are expunged."

"We're working on that—Blake and I," he said. "We've got a plan."

Her eyes lit up. "Thank you, Dad. Honestly, Blake is incredible. I'm so grateful you hired him. He's the smartest man I've ever met... aside from you."

He chuckled. "Sounds like someone's got a crush."

She laughed, wiping at her eyes. "He's a serious upgrade from my last fatal attraction."

Her father shook his head. "I knew Carl was bad news the minute you brought him home for Sunday dinner."

Tears welled again. "I should've listened to you. I never should've gotten involved."

"Water under the bridge, sweetheart."

She hesitated. "Do you know what happened to Carl?"

He nodded grimly. "He got a plea deal. Minimum sentence. He cracked before trial, giving them everything they needed. Sold out his buddy to save his own skin."

Justine's jaw clenched. "He was just as guilty. He knew what they were going to do."

"Sometimes," her father said, "there's no justice in this world."

She looked down at their joined hands. "Maybe not. But one day... maybe I can help change that."

A Mother's Love

On Mother's Day, the inmates who expected to see their children walked around with a permanent smile on their faces. Although she didn't have the opportunity to be a mother, Justine did have one and couldn't wait to see her.

Justine recalled the time she almost had a child. When she told Carl she was pregnant, he wasn't happy.

"Pregnant!" he said. "You're keeping it?"

"Of course!"

"I hope you realize you won't be able to finish law school once you have a baby."

"When *we* have a baby," she corrected.

Carl shrugged.

Keeping the baby meant she would have to delay her dreams of becoming a lawyer. Through a wall of morning sickness, Justine told her parents. They were in the kitchen. Her mother was at the stove, and her father sat at the table, reading the paper.

Ben looked up. "Oh, look what the cat dragged in."

"Justine! What a nice surprise to see you," her mother squealed. "Would you like breakfast? I'm making your favorite. Pancakes."

"No, I'm not feeling very hungry. I guess it's morning sickness."

"Morning sickness?" her father said. "Don't tell me that you're pregnant with that creep's baby." He stared at her belly.

"I'm not having an abortion if that's what you're thinking, Dad."

"That's out of the question," Kathleen said, narrowing her eyes at her husband.

"Why weren't you using birth control?"

"Ben! You know, contraceptives are against the Catholic religion."

He shook his head and went back to reading the paper.

Justine went window shopping with her mom, looking at baby clothes. She held off buying anything since she didn't know if it was a girl or a boy.

"You can buy yellow," the sales clerk said cheerily.

"No, yellow has never been my favorite color, but I *do* like this mobile." Justine wound the music box and watched the little angels circle around white clouds. Unable to resist, she purchased the mobile and set it up on her headboard.

Carl rolled his eyes but softened and stopped telling her to terminate the pregnancy.

Justine fell in love with the idea of being a mother until one morning, she woke up to wetness. When she threw back the cover, her heart nearly stopped. She was lying in a puddle of blood.

*****

Justine passed Sara in the hallway. Just yesterday, the woman had been beaming, ecstatic at the thought of seeing her two children. She talked about them constantly, her eyes lighting up every time she mentioned their names. But today, her eyes were red and swollen.

"What's wrong?" Justine asked gently. "Aren't you excited? You said you'd finally get to hug your kids today."

"They're not coming," Sara muttered. Her voice cracked. "That bastard decided it's in their best interest to keep them out of prison. He's punishing me."

"Why would he do that?"

Sara hesitated, ashamed. "I was an addict. I messed up, but I've been clean. I've been in the drug rehab program for almost a year now." Her lip trembled. "Those are my babies, Justine. By the time I get out, they won't even remember me."

"Maybe we can talk to the warden—"

"What's the point?" she snapped, then quickly softened. "I appreciate it, but I don't want to talk about it anymore."

"I understand. But if you change your mind, I'm here."

Justine watched her walk away, shoulders hunched with sorrow. Her own thoughts drifted to her mother—due to arrive any moment—and maybe her father, too. She felt a flutter of anticipation but tried not to let hope rise too high.

She returned to her cube, trying to pass the time with a book. Laura was there, crouched on the floor over a bucket.

"What's wrong?" Justine asked.

Laura glanced up, pale and sweating. Her eyes were bloodshot. "Can I trust you with a secret?"

Justine hesitated. Secrets in prison came with risk. But Laura looked desperate.

"Okay," she said. "What is it?"

"I think I'm pregnant."

Justine's mouth dropped open. "What makes you think that?"

"I'm two months late. I just know. Oh God, Justine. What am I going to do?" She folded over herself, burying her head between her knees. "I can't let anyone find out."

"Have you told anyone else?"

"No. I've been careful. But I can't hide it forever."

"You need to tell medical. Maybe there's a way to—"

"No! You don't understand. The father's Allen... a guard." She lowered her voice to a whisper. "If this gets out, we're both screwed."

Justine crouched beside her. "You have options. You could have the baby and put it up for adoption."

Laura shook her head violently. "No. I can't carry it. I need to end this."

"Don't even think about going to that woman —
what's her name? The one who gives out dangerous
remedies —"

"I don't have a choice!"

"Yes, you do. But not like that. Please… just give
me a little time. We'll figure something out."

Laura nodded weakly, tears streaking her cheeks.
"Please don't tell anyone."

"I won't. I promise."

She was about to say more when the PA system
blared: **"Morgan, report to the visitation room."**

Justine jumped up. "I have to go." She grabbed a
washcloth, ran it under cold water, and handed it to
Laura. "Here. Rest for a while. I'll be back soon."

She rushed out of the pod, her heart hammering.
Outside the visitation room, families lined up with
children in tow. A drug-sniffing dog was pacing back
and forth in front of them. A small boy, no older than
six, burst into tears at the sight.

Inside, the room buzzed with activity. Children
clung to their mothers or played with the worn toys in
the corner. Some laughed. Others held back tears,
unsure whether they were staying or leaving. Mothers
put on brave faces, pretending it was normal, but
Justine saw the pain in their eyes.

She scanned the crowd, searching.

Her mother wasn't there.

She sat down and tried to steady her breathing.
Maybe traffic was bad. Maybe her parents were
delayed. She folded a napkin into the shape of a fan,
then again, trying to keep her hands busy.

Then she saw Blake walk in.

At first, her face lit up. But the look in his eyes made her stomach twist.

"Blake?" she said, standing. "What are you doing here?"

"Your father sent me," he said softly. He reached out to hug her.

She pulled back, sensing it before he said a word. "Where's my mother?"

"Justine..." Blake gently guided her back to her chair. He sat across from her and took her hand. "Your mother had a heart attack last night. She died in her sleep."

Justine froze. "No. No. That can't be."

"I'm so sorry. Your father wanted to be here, but... he had to make arrangements."

Justine leapt from the chair. "I have to see her. I have to go — she needs me!"

She bolted toward the door.

Two guards intercepted her, grabbing her arms. She thrashed, screaming. "Let me go! Please — I need to see my mom!"

They forced her to the ground, pinning her down as she kicked and sobbed.

Blake stood helplessly, watching as they dragged her away.

Grief

Justine was thrown into solitary confinement — and welcomed it.

She curled into a ball on the hard cot and cried until her eyes swelled shut. Her thoughts drifted to her mother, memories stretching all the way back to when she was four years old. Solitary was the perfect place to relive every second, to replay her mother's voice, her touch, her laugh.

Overwhelmed by guilt, Justine would have given anything to go back to before her rebellious teenage years, to before she lashed out and caused so much pain.

The metal slot on her cell door screeched open.

"Morgan!" a guard barked.

She lifted her head, voice hoarse. "Am I going back to my pod?"

"No. Hands through the slot."

She obeyed, and the cuffs clicked around her wrists. Two guards stepped in, one on either side.

"Where are you taking me?"

"The infirmary."

"But I'm not sick."

At the check-in desk, her case manager, Mr. Labella, was waiting.

"Why am I being taken to medical?"

He sighed. "Don't complain. You'd be in solitary confinement for weeks if it weren't for your lawyer friend. Blake spoke to the warden. Said you were crazed with grief. Just go with it. They'll give you something to calm you down, keep you under observation. After that, you'll be released. It won't even go on your record."

Reluctantly, she nodded. "Please check if I have any mail. I'm expecting books. I need to focus on something — anything — other than losing her."

"I'll look," he said, but his tone was skeptical. "Don't count on doing much studying here."

A nurse led her to a bed and handed her a paper cup.

"Take this."

Justine glanced inside. Three pills — blue, pink, and white.

"What are they?"

The nurse rolled her eyes. "I don't have time for this. Take the damn pills and get in bed, or I'll get the cuffs."

Justine swallowed them reluctantly. The nurse pried open her mouth with a tongue depressor to check, gagging her in the process.

The woman in the next bed turned her head. "Hi, I'm Teresa."

"Justine."

"You don't look sick," Teresa said. "What are you in for?"

"My mother died," Justine said quietly, a sharp ache tightening in her gut.

"I'm sorry. My problems seem small compared to yours."

"What are you here for?"

"Besides being old?" Teresa chuckled. "I have pancreatitis. I applied for compassionate release months ago. I've served more than half my sentence, and I'm dying. My son and his wife even offered to take care of me."

"Did you talk to your case manager?"

"Yeah. He says to be patient."

"There's a chance. You could file directly with the court."

"I didn't know that," Teresa whispered. "I just want them to send me to hospice and let it be done."

"Hospice?"

"A British doctor started it about ten years ago. It's meant to bring dignity to dying inmates. Better than wasting away here."

The meds dulled Justine's senses. Her eyes fluttered closed. "I'll help you... When I get out," she murmured before sleep claimed her.

She woke to the clang of food trays. The room reeked of antiseptic and old sorrow. A television droned on in the background, but no one was watching.

"I didn't realize how many sick inmates there were," she said to Teresa.

"They stash us in a corner and forget we exist. At least they expect nothing. We're free to sleep our lives away."

An orderly wheeled in a cart. The food looked even worse than the regular prison fare—bland, colorless. The meds had her stomach churning, and the smell pushed her over the edge. She vomited into the bedpan beside her tray, shoved it away, and lay back, tears leaking from the corners of her eyes.

Her mother was gone.

And because of her outburst, Justine had been denied furlough. She never even got to say goodbye.

The door creaked, and a man stepped inside.

"Ms. Morgan," he said gently, "I'm a therapist. I've been sent to help you."

She didn't move. "No one can help me. I let her down in life and in death. I didn't get to say goodbye. It's all my fault."

"What is?"

"Prison broke her heart. I killed my mother."

"That's not true. She was sick. You didn't cause this."

"She'd disagree."

"Talking might help."

"I don't want to talk."

"It's not the end of the world, Justine. Time heals all."

"So does a stiff drink," she cut in bitterly. "Are clichés all you've got?"

He smiled softly. "Clichés are just little truths. And here's another—your mother wouldn't want this. She'd want you to live, to thrive."

Justine stared at the ceiling, lips trembling.

"You're a good person," he continued. "You're smart. I heard you're taking law courses."

"I don't care anymore."

"I think you do. What would your mother want?"

Justine's voice was faint. "She'd want me to keep going. To pray more. I've never been good at that."

"Then do it your way. But don't stop. She'll be watching when you graduate."

Justine nodded slowly. "I've been taking correspondence classes... but my brain's too foggy to focus."

"I can take you off the depression meds—if that's what you want. But I'll need to keep you here a few more days to monitor you."

She hesitated.

Then: "Yes. Please. I want to feel something again."

*****

Justine remained in the med unit for seven days.

On her release, instead of heading straight back to her pod, she walked toward the row of payphones. Her feet moved on instinct. She needed something—anything—to anchor her in the world again.

She picked up the receiver and dialed her parents' number. Even though she knew her mother was gone, she had to hear her voice one last time.

The line rang four times.

Then:

"Hello, you've reached the Morgan residence. We're not home right now, but if you leave your name and number, we'll return your call as soon as possible. Have a blessed day."

Her mother's voice. So warm. So familiar. Still alive in this one tiny sliver of space.

Justine pressed the phone tighter to her ear as tears slid silently down her cheeks. When the beep sounded, she whispered, "I love you."

She knew no one would call her back.

The line went dead. She hung up slowly, her fingers trembling, then turned and walked through the corridor like a ghost.

Instead of going back inside, she slipped out to the courtyard. A soft drizzle fell from the gray sky, cool and cleansing. She tilted her face upward and let the rain mingle with her tears.

For a long time, she stood there — alone in the open air — letting her grief wash over her in silence.

Compassion

As promised, Justine began researching the compassionate release program. She was right about one thing: under the First Step Act, federal inmates could petition the courts directly for a sentence reduction, bypassing the Board of Prisons — but only in certain states. Florida wasn't one of them.

Undeterred, she drafted a letter urging lawmakers to add Florida to the list. She cited the high costs of incarcerating elderly, terminally ill inmates and argued that placing them in senior care facilities would be both humane and economically sensible.

It was the only way she could help Teresa — and others like her.

She approached the warden with her concerns.

Mr. Atwood leaned back in his chair, arms crossed. "Only twenty-six inmates have been granted compassionate release in the last five years," he said. "The system's slow. There's a deep reluctance to release inmates, even when better alternatives exist."

"I can't give up," Justine replied. "Someone has to fight for these women. They're at the end of their lives, and no one's even listening."

He studied her for a moment, then nodded. "I applaud your efforts. Maybe you'll be the one to get through. You know what they say — the squeaky wheel gets the grease."

*****

After her release from the medical ward, Justine took a seat at the senior table in the cafeteria. She watched quietly, taking notes as the women around her moved slowly, their minds dulled by years of confinement and inactivity.

At first, no one spoke. Then, like a dam breaking, the complaints came pouring out.

"My bones ache from those thin mattresses."

"I sure wish I had a hearing aid — I can barely hear anymore."

"I need a walker, especially at night when I have to get to the bathroom."

"My teeth are gone. I can't chew anything."

"The food gives me heartburn."

"I can't bathe without help," one woman added in a whisper. "But if they find out how sick I really am, they'll stick me in the hospice corner. I'd rather die in my cell than be lonely and forgotten."

Justine scribbled furiously, overwhelmed by the sheer weight of their struggles. She had known things were bad — but not this bad.

She visited Teresa whenever she could, sneaking into the elder ward when one of the kinder guards was on duty. It was against the rules — technically "out of bounds" — but the CO looked the other way. Teresa, now more stooped and quiet, rarely spoke of her past. Her time was mostly spent curled up on her bunk, lost in silence.

Most of the inmates in the elder unit were over seventy-two, suffering from chronic conditions like heart disease, high blood pressure, or limited mobility. Some were nearly blind. Others shuffled around in silence, their memories fading.

Justine had an idea. These women didn't just need medicine — they needed dignity. A proper elder care unit. Maybe even a nursing home within the prison walls, for those without family or support on the outside. Somewhere safe. Somewhere humane.

She needed help.

Justine picked up the phone and dialed Blake, hoping he would come visit again. Maybe he could help advocate for elderly inmates and take on the cause pro bono. The mission was noble, rooted in justice — but there was something more.

She missed him.

And no matter how hard she tried to stay focused on the work, Justine knew she was falling in love.

*****

At sixty-eight, Carol received the notice: she was being released.

She stood in the hallway, clutching the letter like a death sentence. "This is the only home I've known for forty years."

"They're sending you to a women's shelter," Justine said gently. "You'll be okay, Carol. They'll help you get back on your feet."

Carol gave a sharp shake of her head. "I'd rather be homeless."

Despite her protests, she was loaded into the prison van and driven away. Justine couldn't stop thinking about her—picturing her curled up on park benches, hungry, cold, invisible. Her worry stretched into days, then weeks.

Two weeks later, the news came.

Carol had walked into a department store, calmly stuffed merchandise into her jacket, and lingered beneath the surveillance cameras. She didn't even run when the manager called the police. Just as she'd hoped, they arrested her.

She was back.

Teresa, on the other hand, had been released into the care of her son and his new wife. At first, Justine was hopeful—grateful her friend had a family waiting. But then a letter arrived.

They make me stay in my room. They keep my Social Security checks. If I complain, they scream at me.

Justine's heart dropped. She suspected elder abuse and reported it immediately.

A week later, Teresa was found dead—suffocated, a plastic bag over her head, cinched with one of her scarves.

The grief was unbearable.

Every time Justine tried to help, something went wrong. She had dreamed of creating change, but instead, she was branded a threat.

In the cafeteria, the backlash began.

"Don't talk to her," a steel-haired woman growled. Her jaw was clenched, her face as hard as stone. "She won't be happy until we're all shipped out."

"I'm not trying to hurt you," Justine said, voice trembling. "I just want to make things better. You deserve dignity."

The woman slammed her tray down. "This is *it* for us—our golden years. No one out there gives a damn. We'll all end up on the street or in a box."

Suddenly, Carol stormed across the room. Her eyes blazed as she grabbed Justine by the collar of her khaki shirt.

"You can't keep meddling in the system," she hissed. "You think you're helping, but you're killing us."

She raised her fist.

"Stop it! Or I'll knock you out."

Justine braced herself for the blow.

"Leave her alone," another inmate snapped, stepping between them. "She's just trying to help."

The room fell silent. Justine backed away, her heart pounding.

She wanted to make a difference. But now she wasn't sure if she was fixing anything—or just making everything worse.

Predator

As Justine stepped into the hallway on her way to the library, Officer Allen Murphy intercepted her. His stance was tense, his eyes fixed on hers.

"Can I talk to you?" he asked, already turning toward his office.

She followed reluctantly, her stomach twisting. She suspected this had to do with Laura—and her pregnancy. Sweat prickled the back of her neck.

Once inside, Allen shut the door with a hard click.

"I don't know what you've heard," he started, lighting a cigarette with shaking fingers, "but your cellmate claims I knocked her up."

Justine said nothing.

He exhaled, eyes narrowing. "Some shit is about to hit the fan. I figured I'd give you a heads-up."

"Why me?" she asked.

"Because there are people who might start asking questions."

"About what?"

"You know damn well." His voice dropped, his tone threatening. "I'm not about to lose my job—or my pension—over some piece of ass. You tell your roomie to keep her mouth shut. For her own good."

Justine clenched her fists. She knew better than to get caught between inmates and officers. But this was too much.

"You miserable bastard," she whispered.

Allen stood, looming over his desk. "Careful, prisoner. I could toss you in solitary for that."

"I don't care. That's your child, Laura's carrying, and everyone knows it—including the warden, if I tell him."

"You've got no proof," he snapped, pacing. His eyes darted nervously. "Who else knows?"

His cigarette burned down to his fingers, making him flinch. He dropped it, cursing, and crushed it beneath his boot, leaving a black smear on the floor.

"A DNA test would prove everything," Justine said. "She's only nineteen. You took advantage of her. You're a predator."

Allen's face turned red. He kicked the chair over and raised his fist.

"You touch me," she warned, "and I'll blow the whistle so loud the BOP will hear it in D.C. I'll write letters to every watchdog group in the country."

He froze, then slumped back into his chair. He dropped his head into his hands.

"Get out," he growled.

Justine didn't need to be told twice. She yanked the door open and left.

Later that afternoon, as she passed the supply closet, she heard muffled voices. She paused, leaned in, and pressed her ear to the door.

"Listen, you little bitch," Allen hissed. "No one's gonna believe you. I'm a decorated officer. You're a convict. You'll lose. So you better get rid of it."

"Get rid of it?" Laura's voice broke. "How? What do you want me to do?"

"I don't care. Drink bleach, throw yourself down the stairs. Just make sure you miscarry. You've got until noon tomorrow."

Justine backed away from the door, her heart racing. Moments later, Allen stormed out, wiping his hands on a handkerchief.

When he was gone, Justine slipped into the closet. Laura was curled in a ball on the floor, blood on her lip.

"What am I gonna do?" she sobbed.

Justine crouched beside her. "I don't know. But we'll figure something out."

"I should've grabbed his gun," Laura muttered. "I should've shot him."

"Don't say that," Justine whispered. "Please. Don't think like that."

Laura looked up, eyes full of rage and despair. "What other choice do I have?"

"You can report him. We can go to Mr. Atwood."

"I can't," she said. "I appreciate you trying to help, but... I need to be alone."

"Do you want help getting back to the pod?"

"No. Just... go."

Justine hesitated, torn, then quietly slipped out.

Her hands trembled as she walked. *It can't be right*, she thought. *A guard uses a girl, gets her pregnant, threatens her, and walks away clean?* But deep down, she feared the worst.

*****

The next morning, they found Laura hanging from a shelving unit in the storage room, a sheet tied around her neck.

The prison ruled it a suicide.

But Justine didn't believe it.

Laura had been terrified, yes — but she'd also been defiant. Desperate. Still, something about it felt wrong. Laura had wanted help, not an escape. She would never have harmed her baby.

Before the guards could clear out Laura's belongings, Justine rifled through her cabinet. At the back, inside a plastic bag, she found a pair of panties and a folded slip of paper. On it, Laura had scrawled one word in shaky handwriting:

Proof.

A chill spread through Justine's chest.

Laura had left behind her own evidence — her voice silenced, but her will unbroken.

Gripping the bag, Justine went straight to the warden's office.

"There's no way she hung herself, Mr. Atwood," she said, her voice trembling. "She wouldn't have hurt her baby."

"Baby?" he asked, startled.

"She was pregnant," Justine said. "She didn't want the child, not at first—but she was scared. And in the end, I think… she wanted to keep it."

"Do you know who the father was?"

She hesitated. "Yes. But I'm afraid to say. He threatened me. I don't want to be the next one in the morgue."

"Justine," Atwood said gently. "Do you want your friend's killer to walk free? You have a chance to stop this. I promise you—whatever you tell me stays confidential. I will not allow harm to come to you."

Justine looked down at her shoes. Her pulse pounded in her ears. When she looked back up, her eyes were blazing.

"It was Allen Murphy."

The warden's jaw clenched. "How long?"

"I think it started not long after she arrived. Seven months ago."

"Jesus, Justine. Why didn't you come to me sooner?"

"You don't get it," she snapped. "If I ran in here every time I saw something wrong, I'd be labeled a snitch. Do you know what happens to snitches in here? It's not just bruises—it's blood, isolation, humiliation."

"I understand," he said quietly. "I'll handle this. You have my word. You won't be implicated."

Justine left his office with her stomach in knots and her nerves frayed. A dark sense of dread followed her through the halls.

Mr. Atwood ordered a DNA test on the evidence Laura had left behind. But the process was slow — new technology, backlogged labs. Results could take months.

In the meantime, Allen Murphy was quietly transferred to another facility pending investigation.

As he was escorted out, he passed Justine in the hallway. Their eyes locked. He raised a fist, eyes full of venom.

It sent a jolt of fear straight to her core.

But she stood her ground.

This time, she hadn't stayed silent.

Advocate

A new inmate took Laura's bed.

Her name was Trisha — perky, young, and blonde. Arrested on drug charges, she had recently been transferred to Larsen for its well-regarded rehabilitation program ahead of her release. Her energy was different, nervous but determined.

She took a deep breath, then told Justine her story.

"My ex and I were in the middle of a nasty custody battle over our fourteen-year-old daughter. He had a criminal record and was on probation for domestic abuse, but the family court judge still granted him visitation every other weekend. Threatened to jail me if I didn't comply."

She paused, as if still trying to make sense of it all. "After one visit, my daughter came home and went straight to her room. She wouldn't talk. Then her appetite vanished, and she started sleeping through school. I thought she was depressed."

Justine listened intently.

"Finally, she broke down and told me — he touched her." Trisha's voice cracked. "I reported it to Child Protective Services. They said they'd investigate."

"She's old enough to talk to a judge," Justine said softly.

"Yeah, well, the judge said there was no evidence. Ignored everything I said. And when my ex found out I reported him, he went ballistic. Filed a complaint with DCF, said I planted the idea in her head. Accused me of having Munchausen by proxy. Next thing I knew, CPS took my daughter to a safe house."

Justine's jaw tightened.

"I snapped. I started using again," Trisha admitted, blinking fast. "My sister found me passed out on the bathroom floor. If she hadn't rushed me to the ER, I'd be dead."

"That's awful. Where's your daughter now?"

"She's living with my mom. My lawyer's filing an appeal. He said enrolling in Larsen's drug program would help my case. One of the counselors even agreed to testify."

"He must be good," Justine said. "Most of the women here are locked up for nonviolent drug offenses."

Trisha nodded. "The program's called the Drug Offender Sentencing Alternative. Nonviolent offenders can serve less time if they complete at least ninety days of treatment and stay clean. Then they serve the rest under community supervision."

"Like a halfway house?"

"Sort of. But it's more focused on recovery and mindset. They call them *recovery residences*. You get a personal counselor, attend daily group sessions, and work on the trauma that led you to use in the first place."

"It sounds like a much better solution than locking people up."

"I think so too. But they're strict. One slip and you're out. Fail a drug test, show up late, or skip a meeting—and they send you back."

"Is there a time limit?"

"Yeah. Once you get a job, you pay a portion of your income—up to twenty-five percent. It's a sliding scale. I had a friend who finished the program. She was scared the whole time, but they helped her get stable. She found an apartment and held down a job. It worked."

Justine sat back, absorbing it all. "This could help a lot of people."

Trisha smiled faintly. "You can't fix the whole system, Justine. But maybe... case by case, you could make a difference."

Justine nodded. Now officially named an inmate advocate by Mr. Atwood, she made a mental note to bring up the program with him. If it worked for

Trisha, it could work for others too—and Justine wasn't done fighting.

Logic and Reason

While other inmates were caught up in drugs and gang drama, Justine focused on her studies alongside students from the local college. She had already completed her American Government and Communications requirements. Only a few classes stood between her and her degree — Social Science and the one she'd avoided until the end: Statistics. That's where she met Carl, a quiet, analytical student. She often wondered how different her life might have been if math had come easier to her.

Still, she was glad she'd taken Logic and Reasoning in college. Law schools favored students who could analyze, contextualize, and critique. And Justine loved a good argument.

Her latest debate? Solitary confinement.

Kelly and Carmen — the two inmates who'd set the library ablaze — were finally released back into general population. After six months in segregation, the difference between the two was startling. Carmen seemed relatively unaffected, still chasing risky pleasures like smoking crack in the bathroom and smuggling in contraband. But Kelly... Kelly had changed. She looked like a cornered animal, her wild eyes darting around the room, no longer speaking to her former best friend.

Isolation, Justine thought, might be the worst form of punishment for someone with an unsettled mind. Humans needed voices—conversation, connection. Some were victims of trauma long before they ever saw the inside of a cell. Solitary only made things worse.

She began researching. Statistics showed a rise in isolation use across U.S. prisons, yet there was no proof that it helped. Justine believed solitary was more about satisfying the control of staff than rehabilitating inmates. Without a trial or a jury, the women placed in isolation had no recourse. And the psychological toll— anxiety, depression, even psychosis—was severe.

Still, she couldn't entirely dismiss it. Inmates who posed a genuine threat needed separation. She decided to write her final paper on the subject.

One day, she approached Harry, a guard recently transferred from the solitary wing.

"What's the purpose of solitary?" she asked.

Harry raised an eyebrow. "It's for inmates who are a danger to others. With two thousand women in here, it helps us maintain order."

"But isn't isolation harmful? Doesn't it cause more damage than it prevents?"

"It's been used for centuries," Harry said with a huff. "Back in the 1700s, religious folks used to isolate people with nothing but a Bible. They were supposed to find repentance."

"That doesn't make it right."

"Sometimes inmates need to be alone with their thoughts."

"Some thoughts are dangerous," Justine countered. "And America uses solitary confinement more than any other country. The UN even classifies it as torture."

"The UN sucks," he snapped. "One-world government bullshit."

"It's not about politics. Some states are already limiting or banning it—New York, California."

"Goddamn liberals," Harry muttered, folding his arms.

Justine didn't press further. She had what she needed.

*****

She earned an A on her paper, arguing that solitary confinement was overused and disproportionately applied to nonviolent offenders. Her alternative? A system she called *Carrots and Sticks*—a balance of sanctions and rewards. Even mentally ill inmates, she argued, were given little mercy or support.

She submitted the article to a women's magazine, hoping it might ignite a broader conversation. As Madeleine Albright once said, *"There's a special place in hell for women who don't help other women."*

Fran, another inmate recently accepted into the college program, became her study partner. Justine had seen her around before—quiet, intense. Thirty-six, convicted of assault with a deadly weapon after shooting at her ex-husband.

One afternoon, Justine's curiosity got the better of her.

"Do you mind if I ask... why did you shoot him?"

Fran didn't flinch. "He was a deadbeat dad. Never paid child support, claimed his boss cut his hours—but I knew he was getting paid under the table. Still, the court gave him full visitation. When I tried to protect my kids, the judge warned me about parental alienation."

She paused. "Then one night, Stevil—that's what I call him now—banged on the door. Woke everyone up. I was scared. So I bought a gun. Next time he came around, I fired a warning shot. It hit him in the leg."

Justine winced.

Fran shrugged. "I lost custody after that. He's got the kids now."

"What will you do when you get out on parole?"

"I'll fight for them. But I'll need a job, a place to live. The prison gives you a bus ticket and two hundred bucks in gate money. That's not going to get me far."

"Your caseworker might help get you into a halfway house."

"Maybe. But I've been a stay-at-home mom since the kids were born. I don't even know where to start."

"You're smart, Fran. You're getting your education. You'll figure it out."

Fran smiled faintly. "Thanks, Justine. I hope you're right."

Faith

Six months later, Justine finished her classes and poured herself into her thesis. She titled it *Land of the Free*, a paper examining punishment versus rehabilitation in the American justice system. The irony of the title wasn't lost on her. The binding on her notebook had unraveled from overuse, pages dog-eared and ink-smudged from endless rewrites. She pulled off the stretched rubber band that held it together and flipped to her most recent draft. The words blurred — she couldn't focus.

Her thoughts drifted to Blake. She pictured the dimple in his cheek when he smiled, the warmth in his voice when he called her name. Their Saturday visits were the highlight of her week, moments when the steel bars seemed to vanish. Two more days, she reminded herself, but even that small countdown couldn't tame the nervous flutter in her chest.

Outside her cube, a commotion broke the afternoon lull. Mail call.

She heard her name.

Sliding off the bunk, she rushed to the common area, her heart hopeful. Maybe it was her thesis feedback. Instead, it was a letter from Fran.

Justine tore it open with trembling fingers, expecting to read about new beginnings, second chances, a happy ending.

But her chest tightened as she read the first lines. It wasn't the freedom Fran had imagined. Not even close.

Dear Justine,

I hope you're doing well. As for me, I'm technically free — but it doesn't feel that way. Out from behind bars, but still stuck in a system that doesn't let you breathe.

Every time I think I'm getting somewhere, I hit a wall. Getting a job as a felon is like trying to run with your legs tied. Employers smile in the interview, then ghost you the minute they find out about your record. Landlords? Same thing. I'm still at the women's shelter — four cots to a room, and someone crying every night. It's not home. It's barely survival.

Some days I think about giving up. But then I think of you, and all the times you told me I was smart, that I could do this. I'm trying to hold onto that. I really am.

Your friend,
Fran

Blake and Justine had shared many late-night strategy sessions in the dimly lit prison visitation room. It was during those long hours that she realized she'd fallen for him. Blake wasn't just her lawyer anymore — he was her confidant, her steadying force, her hope in a world that had long stopped offering any.

One Thursday, Justine was unexpectedly summoned to the administration building. Her heart leapt. It wasn't her usual day to see Blake, but something in her gut told her it was him. A guard led her to the council room, unlocked her handcuffs, and disappeared without a word.

Before she could say anything, Blake crossed the room and kissed her.

He smelled of horses, hay, and sawdust — the comforting scent of a simpler world beyond the prison gates. She melted into him, then reluctantly pulled back, glancing nervously at the door.

"If the guard sees us, I could lose my legal privileges," she whispered.

"I know," he said, brushing a hand down her arm. "I just didn't want to wait until Saturday."

She smiled. "I've missed you."

"I've missed you, too."

"But… do you have any news from the appellate court?"

Blake shook his head. "Not yet. They're still reviewing your file."

Justine began to pace. "What's taking so long? The Parole Board recommended my release."

He leaned forward. "The governor's playing it safe. With the election coming up, he's stalling. No one wants to risk appearing soft on crime."

"So it's all politics," she said, her voice laced with bitterness. "It doesn't matter that I'm innocent."

He looked at her tenderly. "You're tired. I can see it in your eyes."

"I just... I don't know how much longer I can hang on, Blake. Maybe I should just accept this life."

"No." He stood and took her hands. "Don't lose faith, honey."

"That's what my mother would have said. 'Hold on to your faith.' But it's hard, Blake. I got a letter from Fran. She's out, but she can't get a job. No one will hire her with a record."

Blake frowned. "It's all too common. I've seen it with my male clients, too. Especially the older ones. The stigma sticks. There's talk of banning criminal history questions on applications, but most places still ask."

"How are they supposed to rebuild their lives?" she said. "Fran is smart. She'd make a great receptionist or work in an office. Do you know anyone who might give her a shot?"

"I might. One of my clients owes me a favor—I'll call him."

"You're such a good man," Justine said softly. "I wish I'd met you before Carl."

Blake gave a wry smile. "Hard to believe you ever gave that guy the time of day."

"I thought he was kind. It wasn't until I was deep under his spell that I saw his true colors."

"Sociopath," Blake said flatly. "They always wear a mask."

"I've made some bad choices, but if I hadn't... I wouldn't have met you."

They talked for the rest of the visit about everything they would do once she was free — small dreams, big plans. A future.

When he touched her cheek again, she kissed him back. This time without hesitation. His sweetness overwhelmed her. As they embraced, she fought the urge to bury her face in his chest and stay there forever.

"I'll be back next week," he promised.

Justine clutched his hand. "I love you."

"Don't worry, honey. I'm going to get you out of here."

Self-Defense

The pastor's wife, Gail, was up for parole again. Last time, it had been denied — despite Justine's help. Back then, she hadn't known all the details. This time, she was determined to build a stronger case.

Justine focused all her energy on Gail's hearing, pushing everything else aside. She dug into the case file, determined to prove a pattern of abuse. She contacted the hospital Gail had visited after the brutal beating from her husband and requested the photos of her injuries — images that had never been introduced at trial. If that evidence had been presented, the outcome might have been different.

Gail had only fourteen days to appeal the conviction, but her original lawyer had dropped the ball. Now, Justine had what that lawyer never did: documented proof that Gail feared for her life. When she stabbed her husband, it was self-defense.

Hours passed as Justine pored over self-defense cases. Her eyes burned from reading; her head ached from strain. When the bell rang for daily exercise, she stepped outside for air.

A slight chill hung in the morning breeze, but the sky was clear and endless. Justine tilted her face toward the sun, soaking in the warmth. Her spirit lifted, and the weight in her chest eased. Renewed, she headed back inside—only to find the air buzzing with excitement.

"What's going on?" she asked a nearby guard.

"The governor's here," he said. "Came to congratulate the warden on the vocational program. They're saying we're a model prison now."

Justine smiled. *Model prison?* "Where are they?"

"In the auditorium."

She hurried to the back of the auditorium and slipped inside just in time to see the governor shaking Warden Atwood's hand. Cameras flashed as a major network news crew captured the moment.

"Mr. Atwood," a reporter asked, "can you tell us why your program has been so successful?"

"Of course," Atwood said, standing tall. "Here at Larsen Correctional Institute, we've transformed our workforce. Inmates now apply for skilled positions within the prison. Every one of them has a chance to succeed—an opportunity to reinvent themselves.

"We offer classes in real-world trades. Before applying for a job, each inmate must pass a final exam in their chosen field. Those selected earn far more than the typical fourteen cents an hour—it's real pay for real work.

"It's paid off. This prison operated in the red for over a decade. This year, we're finally in the black. But the greater reward is the impact on society: reduced recidivism and stronger reintegration."

"Do you have plans for more changes?" the reporter asked.

"Absolutely. In fact, I've recently appointed one of our inmates as an internal advocate. She's a law student and will report to me directly each week."

Justine's heart skipped.

Is he talking about me?

The camera panned over the crowd. She stayed hidden in the back, uncertain whether to be proud or terrified.

But after launching her campaign for reform, there was no turning back. Not now. Not when Mr. Atwood was riding a wave of publicity — and counting on her to help carry it forward.

*****

Justine sat across from Gail in the common area, her manila folder thick with notes and documents. She opened it and gently slid two photographs across the table.

Gail gasped.

Her right eye was swollen shut, her jaw stitched and caked with dried blood. The images dragged old memories to the surface — ones she had buried deep. She turned her face away, trembling.

"Where did you get these?" she whispered.

"I requested them from the hospital," Justine said softly. "I know it's hard to look at, but they could be the key to winning your parole hearing. The records back you up—it was self-defense. The nurse's notes even state that you were terrified, too afraid to press charges because he threatened to kill you."

Gail's voice cracked. "No one wanted to stand up to him. He was a pastor. Maybe they thought going against him would land them in hell."

Justine leaned in. "That's not all. I found something else—something the court overlooked."

Gail's eyes flickered with a faint spark. "What is it?"

"Florida has a law called *Stand Your Ground*. It protects people who believe they're in immediate danger. When you were tried, *you* had to prove it was self-defense. But the law's changed—now, it's up to the prosecution to prove it *wasn't*."

"I—I don't understand. So what does that mean for me?"

"It means you have a strong chance," Justine said. "I've drafted an argument that your lawyer failed you, that critical evidence was ignored, and that the legal burden has shifted. These photos alone show how much danger you were in."

Gail's hands trembled in her lap. "What if I fall apart in there? I get emotional just thinking about it."

"You're stronger than you think," Justine said gently. "But during the hearing, you have to stay calm. Show them you're stable. They'll be watching everything—your tone, your body language. Don't give them any reason to doubt you."

Gail gave a small, uncertain nod. "Thank you, Justine. I don't know how you do it. But I'm glad you're doing it for me."

Alternative Sentencing

Justine knocked on the warden's office door.

"Who is it?" came the gruff voice inside.

"It's Justine. Sorry to bother you. Do you have a minute?"

"Come in, come in." Mr. Atwood cleared a stack of files from the guest chair. "Have a seat."

"Congratulations on your achievement award," she said.

"Thank you. The prison system's finally getting the attention it deserves."

"It wouldn't have happened without your leadership."

He exhaled with a dry chuckle. "There were times I wanted to quit. Working in a place like this, you grow numb. But lately, I've seen some light."

"Things are changing," Justine said. "You've helped shift the culture."

"It's a start, but we're not there yet. That's why I need people like you—eyes and ears inside the trenches. So much goes unnoticed."

"I'm honored to help," she said. "But I've made some enemies."

"That comes with the job. Not everyone likes change. Some of the staff resent it."

"Like Guard Marsh?"

Atwood's brow lifted. "What do you know about Marsh?"

"He's not subtle. He thinks I'm stirring things up — called me a troublemaker."

"Marsh comes from a military background. Order above all else. He's been gunning for my job since the day he arrived. Doesn't like the direction we're heading."

"I'd hate to see all this progress unraveled."

"So would I. I'm watching him."

Justine shifted in her seat. "I wanted to talk to you about something else. My cellmate is part of the new drug offender sentencing alternative. It's a step in the right direction."

"Yes, the DOSA program. It's proof that reform is possible."

"It is, but it doesn't apply to women already sentenced. That doesn't seem fair."

"What are we supposed to do? Open the gates and let everyone out?"

"No, but the vast majority of women here are nonviolent drug offenders. They deserve the same opportunity."

He leaned back, folding his arms. "You're not wrong. Women are the fastest-growing population in prison — and drugs are usually the cause."

"That's why we need incentives. I've been researching a program in Ohio — Tapestry. It's outpatient-based, but it addresses the root causes of addiction. Trauma. Family breakdown. Poverty. The women leave not just clean, but changed."

Atwood sighed, rubbing his temples. "Try selling that to the public. They already think we're too soft. They want punishment, not healing."

"There are other forms of accountability," Justine pressed. "Rehabilitation doesn't mean getting off easy. It means making sure they don't come back."

"The problem is deeper. Punishment and rehabilitation are two opposing philosophies. They've been battling it out for decades."

"But we're treating symptoms, not causes. That's why change is slow. Look at the stats. The programs that work — really work — reduce recidivism. Isn't that what we all want?"

Atwood studied her for a moment. "You've got fire, Justine. You always did." He pulled off his glasses. "Maybe... if you can get the churches involved, we could build something similar to Tapestry here. Faith-based groups can raise support where the government falls short."

"I'll look into it — after finals," she said, smiling.

"How's the thesis coming?"

"I'm calling it *Land of the Free*. A comparison between punitive and restorative justice systems. Did you know that in Australia, they treat crime as an offense against *society*, not just the state? They focus on resolution, not just retribution. Meanwhile, we tear families apart, sending inmates hundreds of miles from their children."

"We're a throwaway society," he muttered.

She nodded. "But we don't have to be."

"And your appeal?"

"I think I'm close. My attorney's hopeful."

"That's great news—for you." He paused, then added with a smirk, "But what if I don't let you go?"

Her eyes widened.

"I could charge you with something else." He grinned. "Kidding. I'm going to miss you, that's all."

"I'll be back," Justine said. "This is only the beginning. Advocacy is my calling."

"I believe that." Atwood leaned forward, more thoughtful now. "I'll give the residential treatment idea some serious thought. Maybe we can pilot something with a halfway house."

"Thank you," Justine said, rising from her chair. "You won't regret it."

Prison Riot

The issue of incarcerating drug-addicted women continued to gnaw at Justine. Two weeks had passed since she'd pitched the idea of alternative sentencing to Mr. Atwood. Though he promised to look into options for already-sentenced inmates, she couldn't shake the feeling that more could be done — right now.

She thought of Trisha, her cellmate in the drug treatment program, and headed straight back to the pod.

"When's your next meeting?" Justine asked.

"This afternoon at two," Trisha said, eyeing her curiously. "Why?"

"I want to sit in on it — with you. Maybe I can make a case to the counselors, see if any of the women might qualify for early release."

Trisha smirked. "What makes you think they'll listen to *you*?"

"They know the women. They might at least consider recommending someone. I'm not saying we'll change the world — but it's a start."

"We?" Trisha raised both hands. "Oh no. I keep my head down and do my time. You stir things up, you make enemies. And some of these girls? They don't play."

"I can't promise nobody will come after you, but think about the women who could benefit. Women like you."

Trisha hesitated, then sighed. "Fine. I'll save you a seat."

Justine arrived early. She mingled with a few familiar faces, then slipped into an aisle seat.

A woman in her mid-forties with streaks of gray in her ponytail approached. "Anyone sitting here?"

"I'm saving it for someone," Justine said, "but I can move over if you'd like."

"Appreciate it." The woman dropped a clear plastic bag to the floor and nudged it under her chair with her foot.

"What landed you here?" Justine asked, casually.

The woman glanced at her sideways, guarded. "Why do you want to know?"

"I didn't mean to pry," Justine said. "I'm just trying to figure out if prison is really solving the drug problem."

The woman's eyes narrowed. "I'm not here because I'm an addict. I was *framed*."

"Framed?"

"My ex found out I was cheating on him. He planted drugs in my car."

"Were you using?"

"Not then. When we first got together, sure. We both used. But I cleaned up once I found out I was pregnant. At first, he was decent. Then he started drinking heavily. Got mean. Verbally abusive. Next day, he'd act like nothing happened."

"Why didn't you leave?"

"I tried. But when I found out I was pregnant again, I stayed—hoping fatherhood might change him. It didn't. I focused on being a mom. I even started working in the school cafeteria when my son went full-day. That's when I met Lewis. One thing led to another. I know it was wrong, but I was lonely. Ryan found out. Next thing I know, I'm driving home from the grocery store, and there are flashing lights in my rearview."

Her voice hardened. "Cops pull me over. Search the car. Find pot—which I'll admit was mine—but also a bag of coke hidden under the passenger seat. I *never* touched that stuff. Ryan planted it."

"That's awful," Justine said.

"I've got a good lawyer, though. He found witnesses who said my ex bragged about 'sending me up the river.' I've got a hearing for a new trial next month."

Justine nodded. "I'll be rooting for you."

"Thanks," the woman said, her tone softer now. "We all need someone in our corner."

*****

As Justine sifted through statutes, legal cases, and journal articles, a pattern emerged: mass incarceration wasn't working. The spike in crime during the 1970s and '80s led to a movement demanding harsher punishments. Drug-related offenses were blamed for the rise in violent crime, and in response, lawmakers enacted strict sentencing guidelines. "Three Strikes and You're Out" became the law of the land.

Though crime rates briefly dipped, the long-term result was a system caught in a cycle of reoffending and overcrowding. The same offenders returned again and again — untreated, unrehabilitated. Justine shook her head. Higher costs. Fewer results. Her conclusion was clear: the prison system was obsolete.

An announcement crackled over the PA system.

"Attention: All inmates. A meeting will be held in the auditorium at 3 p.m. regarding a new drug rehabilitation initiative. Interested parties should attend."

Justine snapped her book shut and leapt off her bunk. *This is really happening.*

She found Laura already seated in the auditorium and took the chair beside her.

Mr. Atwood stepped to the podium. "It's come to my attention," he began, "that ten to twenty percent of inmates currently incarcerated for drug offenses could be safely reintegrated into society with proper treatment."

He scanned the room. "The new program will require inmates to remain drug-free for at least one year. At that point, eligible participants may transition to a residential facility in lieu of serving the remainder of their sentence behind bars."

A skeptical voice rose from the front row. "Who's gonna pay for all this?"

"Funding will come from the Second Chance Act," Mr. Atwood explained. "We'll prioritize non-violent offenders. This initiative includes a 'pay-it-forward' model. Those who graduate from the program will be expected to mentor others."

Another inmate shouted, "What if we mess up?"

"You'll be returned to prison," he said plainly. "But this isn't about punishment. It's about rehabilitation. While you'll still be under the jurisdiction of the federal prison system, you'll enter an Intensive Supervision Program—ISP."

From the back, someone scoffed. "Sounds like boot camp. What's in it for us?"

"The benefits are real," Atwood said firmly. "This is a path out of incarceration. You'll work with counselors, churches, and your families to secure housing and jobs. Stay clean, and your children will be eligible for full college scholarships. That's a chance to break the cycle—for good."

A murmur of hope rippled through the room—but not everyone was on board.

Outside, a small group of inmates who weren't serving time for drug offenses began to protest. Two women convicted of larceny shoved their way in. A guard moved to intercept them.

"Get out!" he ordered.

Sally, the larger of the two, spun and punched him square in the face. Blood sprayed from his nose as he collapsed. She raised her boot to stomp him, but another guard tackled her to the floor, pinning her in a headlock while a third snapped on handcuffs.

The crowd erupted. Protesters shouted and surged toward the stage. A few broke into the supply closet, grabbing whatever they could — folders, bottled water, extension cords.

Justine dropped to her knees as a shrieking alarm split the air.

"ON THE FLOOR! FACE DOWN!"

The prison went into full lockdown.

From her prone position, Justine glanced toward the back of the auditorium. Guard Marsh stood near the entrance — watching. Not moving. Not helping.

Her heart pounded. The warden's new program was a breakthrough — but it had just sparked a riot. And Justine knew: real change never came without resistance.

Fiona

It was a gloomy Saturday. Justine paced the courtyard, glancing up at the gray sky. She was anxious — Blake was never late.

As the clouds thickened, so did her thoughts.

Why isn't he here? Maybe he's hurt. No, I'd have heard something. Maybe he doesn't love me anymore.

Growing restless, she called him.

"Hi, Justine," Blake answered. "I'm so sorry I couldn't make it today. I'm buried in a case."

"Can you tell me about it?"

"It involves algorithmic sentencing scores."

"I read something about that. They claim to predict the likelihood of future crimes."

"Exactly. *Claim* is the keyword — it's dangerously flawed." His voice was tight. "My client's a Black man in his mid-forties with prior thefts, none violent. But the judge is using an algorithm to justify maximum sentencing. It's like being punished for something you haven't even done."

"You think it's because he's Black?"

"Most likely. These scores factor in age, race, criminal history... and they strip judges of discretion. Some judges are fine with that. They can hide behind the algorithm if it goes wrong."

"Can you help him?"

"I think so. I found data showing where these systems fail, plus a report by a newsroom that proved the bias. White offenders scored lower—even with worse records."

"Can you go public with it?"

"Not yet. I don't want to antagonize the judge. I'm hoping to sway him with the facts."

"You're brilliant."

"I'm just doing my job."

"No—you're more than that. When I get out, we'll work together. We'll fight injustice side by side. We're going to be a hell of a team."

"You'll be free soon. We'll get married and start a family."

Justine hesitated. "I want to be your wife—but I'm not ready for children. Not yet. I need to do this work. Helping women in prison... It's a calling."

"We'll talk more next Saturday. I've got a meeting with the court clerk on Thursday about your appeal."

"Do you think it'll go my way?"

"That's what we're aiming for. Don't lose hope. I'm good at what I do."

"You sound tired."

"I am. That's why I stayed behind today. I just didn't have the strength. I wish there were a way to let you know."

"You could've called Mr. Atwood. He would've passed on a message."

"Didn't think of that. Next time, I will."

"I love you, Blake."

"I love you, too."

She hung up and sat quietly for a moment, thinking. *He's kind, decent, determined...* But her thoughts drifted. *What if I disappoint him? What if I can't give him the life he wants?*

There wasn't time to dwell. She had work to do — final edits on her thesis. Mr. Atwood had agreed to review it with her, so she paid him a visit.

"Come in," he called when she knocked.

"Mr. Atwood, do you have a minute?"

He waved her in and cleared a chair. "What's on your mind?"

"I wanted to thank you — and talk about my thesis. I've been reading this piece called *Beyond the Prison Bubble*. It talks about what happens *after* incarceration."

He nodded. "Big topic."

"I've done the research. Recidivism's out of control. Even with reforms, people leave prison with nothing."

"Haven't I been trying to fix that?"

"You have. But you're meant for more. You could be changing the system on a much larger scale."

He smiled. "That's why I'm running for a commissioner's seat on the state prison board."

"That's perfect! But we can't stop at releasing nonviolent offenders. They need jobs. Housing. They need support."

"That's hard when private businesses can legally turn them away."

"But we *chose* to take their freedom. Doesn't society owe them a shot at survival? Government agencies could hire former inmates. They could do clerical work—at the DMV, Social Security, housing offices."

Mr. Atwood rubbed his chin. "They'd earn a wage and stay off welfare rolls."

"Exactly. But right now, dozens of jobs are closed to them. They can't even get food stamps or housing subsidies in many states. How are they supposed to provide for their families?"

"You really do get it."

"We need accountability. Haven't you read *The Little Prince*?"

He chuckled. "Can't say I have."

Justine smiled. "It's about a boy who learns that when you tame something—when you take responsibility for it—you become responsible for it forever."

Mr. Atwood leaned back in his chair. "That's a lesson a lot of people in this system still need to learn."

*****

Things had been going smoothly for Justine—maybe *too* smoothly. Some inmates took notice, and not everyone was pleased. Gang activity in the common areas was on the rise. Groups of habitual offenders stuck together, enforcing their own twisted version of justice. Most inmates knew better than to challenge them.

Fiona was the worst of the bunch.

Short and wiry, the Brazilian made up for her height with venom. Her sharp tongue and colder stare could unnerve even the most hardened inmates. She led a pack of women who obeyed her every command.

From the start, Fiona had it out for Justine.

One evening, as Justine headed to the bathroom with her toiletries, she found her path blocked.

"This bathroom is closed," one of Fiona's girls sneered. "You'll have to wash off your stink in another pod."

Justine's stomach tightened, but she stood her ground. "You don't own the showers."

Fiona stepped forward. "Oh, you can shower… but it'll cost you."

"You're going to charge me to *take a shower*?"

"A rich bitch like you must have commissary to burn. If you don't have cash, hand over your goods."

"I haven't received my monthly stipend yet."

Fiona's eyes flicked to the clear plastic bag in Justine's hand—soaps, powders, a small bottle of shampoo.

"What's in the bag?" she asked.

Justine clutched it tighter.

Fiona gave a small nod, and her girls closed in.

A sudden, blinding pain shot through Justine's leg—someone had kicked her shin. She cried out, staggering, then hit the floor hard. Arms flew up to protect her face as boots rained down—her ribs, her stomach, her back. Then... blackness.

When she opened her eyes, they were gone.

So was her bag.

She crawled into a stall, retching into the toilet. Each heave sent lightning bolts of pain through her ribs. She gasped for breath, but saw no blood.

Back in her cube, she lay curled up on her bunk, bruised and shaking. She didn't leave except to eat. Even then, she kept her head down and her back to the wall.

She debated reporting the attack to Mr. Atwood, but she knew better. Fiona had eyes everywhere. A snitch wouldn't last long.

From then on, Justine never went to the showers or toilets alone. Survival, in here, meant choosing your battles—and knowing when silence was the only defense.

Graduation

Justine's graduation took place the first week of June. The morning air was still cool with dew, but the sun was already climbing, heating the courtyard inch by inch. Justine's father stood beside Blake, both of them beaming with pride.

Four other women were graduating alongside her. The warden had approved a makeshift platform in the courtyard, and folding chairs had been arranged for families and guests. Even within the confines of barbed wire and concrete walls, Justine felt like a debutante stepping into a new chapter of her life.

Mr. Peterson called each graduate to the stage. One by one, they crossed the platform, received their diplomas, and shook hands with the warden before rejoining their families. When it was Justine's turn, she walked with purpose, her heart thudding in her chest. From the edges of the courtyard, dozens of inmates lined up behind the chain-link fences to watch. Some clapped and cheered. Others sneered and muttered under their breath.

A keynote speaker from *Hope for Prisoners* addressed the crowd, speaking passionately about the power of education to transform lives. He outlined initiatives — workshops, vocational training, mentorships — that aimed to give inmates a real shot at redemption. "When faith communities, mentors, and families rally around returning citizens," he said, "they give them more than support — they give them trust."

Justine listened with rapt attention, inspired but grounded. A law degree, after all, was just the first step. The next was the Bar exam — and it wasn't guaranteed. With her criminal record, the odds weren't in her favor. Ethical rules were strict, and many applicants with felonies were denied. But she had researched cases of ex-inmates who fought for the right to practice law — and won.

And she had Blake.

He'd believed in her from the beginning, when no one else would. He had fought tirelessly for her appeal, and now, as she held her diploma in hand, she knew this wasn't the end of her journey.

It was the beginning.

After the ceremony, Justine stood off to the side with Blake and her father. The guards gave them a rare window of privacy. Her father's eyes were misty as he gripped her shoulders.

"I always knew you were meant for something big," he said, his voice thick. "Even as a little girl, you'd argue your way out of bedtime. You could've been a lawyer back then."

Justine laughed, and for a moment, the prison walls faded from view. "Thank you, Dad. For coming. For everything."

He pulled her into a tight hug. "I'm so proud of you. Don't let anyone tell you that your past defines you. You're rewriting it every day."

Blake stood nearby, watching them with a quiet smile. When her father stepped away to speak with another guest, Blake moved closer.

"You were incredible up there," he said, brushing a strand of hair from her face. "You walked across that stage like you owned the place."

She gave a nervous laugh. "Some of the inmates didn't seem to agree."

He glanced toward the fence, where Fiona leaned against the chain links, her arms crossed, eyes fixed on Justine like a hawk watching prey.

"You've made waves," Blake said quietly. "And when people don't want to rise, they try to pull others down. Stay focused."

"I will. It just… sometimes feels like walking a tightrope. One wrong move…"

"You won't fall," he said. "I'm not letting you."

She looked into his eyes. "You still think I'll be allowed to take the Bar?"

"I don't just think it—I know it. If they deny you, I'll take it all the way to the Supreme Court if I have to."

Justine smiled, touched by his unwavering belief in her. But over his shoulder, Fiona and her girls were still watching.

As the guests began to leave and the graduates returned to their respective pods, Justine lingered in the courtyard, one hand gripping her diploma. It was more than paper. It was proof of resilience, of growth, of possibility.

But freedom wasn't guaranteed. And neither was safety.

When she turned to go back inside, Fiona stepped into her path.

"Lawyer girl," she said with a smirk. "You think you're something now?"

Justine held her gaze, heart pounding, but voice steady. "I don't think—I know."

Fiona's smile vanished.

"Just remember," she said, low and cool, "not everyone in here is clapping for you."

With that, she turned and walked off, her entourage following like shadows.

Justine didn't flinch. She squared her shoulders and stepped forward.

One foot in front of the other. Always forward.

Turn of Events

Guard Simpson, a six-foot-four African American known to everyone as a gentle giant, barked over the PA system in his usual gruff tone. Justine usually tuned him out — until she heard her name.

He poked his head into her cubicle. "Justine, follow me."

"Where are we going?"

"Admissions and Departures."

"Am I going home?"

"No, you're going to court."

"But I don't have clothes."

"Someone will provide clothes at the courthouse."

Her heart thudded in her chest as she climbed onto the prison bus. After two long years, she was finally getting a new hearing. She tried not to let hope in — but maybe, just maybe, today could change everything.

At the courthouse steps, Blake and her father were waiting. She longed to run into their arms, but the shackles around her ankles made even walking a struggle.

"Please," she whispered to the female officer escorting her. "That's my family. Can I talk to them, just for a second?"

"Make it quick. We can't linger outside."

Acid churned in her stomach as the officer led her forward.

"I'm scared, Blake," she said, her voice trembling.

"I know, honey. But it's almost over," he said gently. "Just remember—stay calm. No matter who testifies or what they say. Composure is everything."

"I feel sick. I can't go in front of the judge wearing this uniform."

"Don't worry," her father said, handing a small bag to the guard. "I brought clothes."

Blake's eyes narrowed as he noticed her arm. "What happened there?"

"I fell out of my bunk a few nights ago," she said. "Probably had a nightmare."

"From a distance, it looks like a tattoo," Blake said. "You need to cover it. The judge notices everything. You want to look like the girl next door—plain, proper, and put together. We'll see you inside."

The officer opened a side door and led her to a private bathroom so she could change.

Justine stepped inside, her heart pounding as she unzipped the plain prison jumpsuit. She stared at her reflection in the mirror above the sink. Harsh fluorescent light exposed the dark circles under her eyes and the healing bruise on her arm. She touched it gently, remembering the sting of Fiona's boot, the humiliation of crawling back to her bunk, and the decision not to report it.

She reached into the bag her father had sent and pulled out the carefully folded clothes: a simple cream blouse, a knee-length navy skirt, pantyhose, and low heels. The kind of outfit she might have worn to church before her arrest. She changed quickly, smoothing the skirt with trembling hands. Then she pulled on a cardigan to cover the bruise and whispered to her reflection, "*Girl next door. Stay composed.*"

A knock on the door startled her.

"Let's go," the officer said.

She stepped out, her heart hammering as she walked down the sterile hall. Each step echoed like a drumbeat. Her shackles were gone now, but the weight of what lay ahead made her legs feel heavy.

She entered the courtroom. Silence swallowed her. A few people turned to look—strangers, perhaps reporters. Blake stood as she came in, his eyes meeting hers with quiet encouragement.

The judge, a stern woman in her sixties, adjusted her glasses and glanced over a file.

"Ms. Morgan," she said, her voice firm but not unkind. "Today, we are here to review the motion for a new trial, based on claims of ineffective counsel and newly discovered evidence. Are you prepared?"

"Yes, Your Honor," Justine said, her voice steady despite the storm inside her.

Blake rose beside her.

"Your Honor, we intend to show that Ms. Morgan's original trial was flawed in several critical ways. We will present documentation and testimony proving that key evidence was withheld or ignored, and that bias played a role in both the prosecution and sentencing."

As the proceedings began, Justine sat beside Blake, her hands clasped tightly in her lap. Witnesses were called. New evidence entered the record. A forensics expert testified that the surveillance footage used to convict her had been altered—something her original attorney never challenged. A woman who had once been too afraid to speak now gave a statement under oath, describing how Carl—the real culprit—had confessed to setting Justine up to protect himself.

By the time the judge called for a recess, Justine's head was spinning. She stepped into the hallway and spotted her father through the glass. He gave her a shaky thumbs-up and wiped his eyes with a handkerchief.

Blake touched her shoulder.

"You're doing great. One more push, and we might finally get the ruling we've been fighting for."

Justine nodded, her throat tight. "I'm ready."

She was taken to a small room.

"I'll bring you some food," the guard said, locking the door behind her.

A few minutes later, she returned with a sandwich and a Coke.

"Can I get a bottle of water?" Justine asked. "I don't drink soda."

"Sure. I'll be right back."

She had no appetite, but she nibbled on the bread. The guard never returned with her water. She took a sip of the soda. It was warm and tasted like syrup.

A different guard arrived to escort her back to the courtroom.

She took her seat as Blake stepped to the podium to deliver his closing argument.

"The polygraph test proved she was telling the truth. It wasn't presented during her trial, but her lawyer knew of its existence. The public defender who represented her was inadequate and ignored the facts. He didn't attempt to mitigate her role in the burglary. For this reason, we have filed a writ of habeas corpus to challenge the guilty verdict."

"Does the defendant have anything to add?" the judge asked.

Justine looked toward her father. He smiled as if to say, *You got this.*

She stood and took a deep breath. "Your Honor, I appreciate the opportunity to stand here today. Your willingness to grant this hearing gives me hope. At my first sentencing, I felt it was unfair to be held accountable for someone else's actions."

"Ms. Morgan, you participated in the crime by driving the getaway car."

"Yes, Your Honor, but it was under duress. My boyfriend was abusive. He screamed at me to drive, and I panicked. I was more afraid of him than of the consequences."

The judge flipped through the file. "I see you've been quite active during your incarceration. The warden submitted a letter commending your character and recommending release."

She removed her glasses and offered a small smile. "Thank you, Ms. Morgan. You may be seated. It will take a few days to review this case and issue a final decision. In the meantime, you will return to the institution."

Two guards handcuffed and shackled Justine and led her from the courtroom before she could speak to Blake.

"I'll come to see you soon!" he called after her.

Justine's father rushed to the back of the courtroom. "Can I hug my daughter?"

The guard looked at him for a moment. "I guess that would be all right."

Her father pulled her close and kissed her forehead.

"You did great," he whispered. "I'm proud of you."

"We have to go," the guard said.

"I love you, Dad."

"I love you, too."

They transported Justine back to prison. She was frisked by a guard who ran his fingers over her crotch and breasts, checking for contraband. It was dehumanizing—but not worth filing a complaint and losing her prison privileges.

A Sad Goodbye

The next morning, a guard appeared at Justine's cubicle.

"Morgan, the warden wants to see you in his office."

Her stomach clenched. She had been avoiding Mr. Atwood ever since Fiona and her crew began targeting her. The last thing she needed was for them to think she was getting special treatment — it would only make things worse.

Still, she followed the guard and knocked lightly on the warden's door. "You wanted to see me, Mr. Atwood?"

"Come on in," he said, his tone unusually upbeat. "Shut the door and have a seat."

She sat across from him, tense. He stared at her for what felt like forever. There was something different in the air, and she held her breath.

"I've got good news, Justine," he said at last. "I've been offered the position of corrections commissioner. I'll be leaving Larsen Correctional."

Her eyes widened. "That's wonderful," she said sincerely. Then her voice cracked. "But what will I do without you?" Tears welled up. "I don't think I can handle this place on my own."

He held up a hand, smiling. "I'm not finished. I also received a report this morning." He paused for dramatic effect. "The judge overturned your guilty verdict. You're going home."

"I'm... free?"

"Yes. As soon as the paperwork is processed."

Still in disbelief, Justine asked the nearest CO if she could make a phone call before returning to her cell.

She dialed Blake's number. It rang three times, then went to voicemail.

"Blake," she said into the receiver, hoping he'd pick up. But he didn't. Behind her, a woman on the phone line sighed dramatically.

"Are you gonna stay on all day? People are waiting."

Justine hung up and made her way back to her cubicle. Her roommate, Sara, was stretched out on the top bunk, reading.

"I have news," Justine said, breathless. "The judge overturned my conviction. I'm getting out."

Sara's book dropped to her lap. "Oh, Justine! I'm so happy for you." Then her voice wavered. "But I'm going to miss you. I don't have any other friends in here. Not one."

Justine reached for her hand. "We'll stay in touch. Let's make a pact—no matter what."

Sara nodded quickly. "Yes, I'd like that. Maybe if I ever get out, we can go for lunch. Or shopping."

Justine smiled. "Done. And since I'm leaving, you can have all my stuff. I'm not taking any of it with me."

Sara hesitated. "There is one thing you can give me."

"What is it?"

She looked away, biting her lip. "I know I don't have a right to ask. You'll have your own life again, but... do you think you could check on my children? I just need to know they're okay."

Justine hesitated. She knew the risks—if Sara's husband called it stalking, she could end up right back inside.

"I'll find a way," she said quietly.

Tears filled Sara's eyes. "Thank you, Justine. You're a good friend."

*****

A week later, the paperwork was complete.

Justine took her final walk down the corridor. As she passed the common area, she spotted Fiona sitting at a table in the corner, arms crossed, lips curled in a sneer.

It was a final reminder: some people take pleasure in cruelty. Some people never change.

Outside, the warden stepped out to say goodbye.

"Well, Justine, you did it," he said. "I'll be honest— when you first came here, I thought you were delusional. But you proved me wrong. I'm glad."

Sara appeared at the gate to see her off. She hugged Justine and slipped a handmade paper flower necklace over her head.

"Don't worry, Sara," Justine whispered. "I'm leaving prison, but I won't forget about you."

Release

It was still dark outside when Justine Morgan walked out of the prison gates as a free woman. The air was cool and quiet, yet the weight of her emotions felt heavy and bright all at once. Blake stood just beyond the perimeter, his eyes lit with a mix of relief and joy. As soon as she stepped into the early morning light, he rushed to her and pulled her into a hug that felt like the beginning of everything new.

"You're free, Justine. You're really free," he whispered, holding her close.

"Thanks to you, Blake." Their kiss—long and deep—was the first without the eyes of guards, inmates, or courtrooms. Justine clung to him for a moment, soaking in the warmth and safety of his arms before finally stepping back.

"Let's get out of here," Blake said, opening the passenger door of his BMW.

As they drove off, Justine stared out the window, watching the sun rise above the razor wire that had marked the edge of her world for the past three years.

"I'm sure your father's anxious to see you."

She hesitated. "I'm not sure I'm ready to go home just yet. I need a little time to breathe, to feel this. Maybe we could grab something to eat... take a drive?"

"Absolutely. There's a place called Avalon's — right on the beach."

"That sounds perfect. I miss putting my toes in the sand. Can I borrow your phone? I should let my father know I'll be home later. I don't want him to worry."

"Of course. It's in the glove compartment."

As they made their way toward the restaurant, they passed a neighborhood park. Justine's eyes widened.

"Stop!" she shouted.

Startled, Blake pulled over. Before he could turn off the engine, Justine was already out the door, running toward the open green space. The scent of freshly cut grass filled her lungs. She wanted to lie down and press her body into the earth — but a group of children was playing nearby, and she didn't want to startle them.

Instead, she grabbed Blake's hand. "Let's go on the swings."

"Anything you want, honey."

They strolled to the swing set, arms linked. Justine took everything in like she was seeing the world for the first time — every bird call, every breeze, every shimmer of morning light. She paused, suddenly self-conscious, but then realized: there was no one to stop her anymore. No more boundaries.

At Avalon's, she stared at the menu, overwhelmed. The mingling scents of grilled seafood, citrus, and rosemary filled the air, each one more enticing than the last.

"Everything looks so good," she said.

"I have an idea," Blake offered. "Let's order a bunch of appetizers and try a bit of everything."

"That sounds great. You've been here before—go ahead and choose."

Blake nodded, slipping on his reading glasses. When the waitress came to the table, he looked up. "I think we're ready."

He proceeded to order every appetizer on the menu.

The waitress laughed, tapping the selections into her notepad. "That's a lot of food."

"We're celebrating," he said. "And we want the full experience. Oh—and a bottle of Chablis, please."

"Coming right up."

When the wine arrived, Justine sipped slowly, letting the chilled liquid swirl across her tongue. After two glasses, she felt light—giddy, almost human again. The food came, platter after platter, and she tasted everything with joy, savoring each bite as if it might disappear.

After lunch, they walked along the beach, hand in hand, watching the waves roll in as the sun began its descent.

"Tell me about your family," she asked gently. "You don't talk much about them."

Blake hesitated. "My father was a woodsman. He grew up in rural Pennsylvania and never had much schooling. That's probably why he was so determined for his sons to get an education."

"Sons? You have a brother?"

He paused, then looked out at the water. "It's getting late. Your dad's waiting."

Justine sensed the subject was closed and didn't press.

Blake drove her to her father's house and pulled up at the curb.

"Are you coming in?" she asked.

"No, you need some time alone with your dad. I'll pick you up tomorrow. I have a surprise planned."

"A surprise?"

"Just bring a change of clothes and a bathing suit."

She smiled and kissed him. Behind the curtain, the fabric twitched.

"My father's watching," she laughed. "I'll see you in the morning."

As Blake's car rolled away, she stood for a moment on the sidewalk, smiling to herself. *I'm free.*

Inside, her father met her at the door. "I'm so happy you're home, Justine."

"It's good to be back, Dad. I'm sorry if I worried you. After being locked up for so long, I just needed some fresh air. Blake took me to the beach."

"I understand. It'll take time to readjust."

"I want to get back to work soon."

Ben frowned. "Take it one step at a time. Think logically, sweetheart. Give yourself space to settle."

"You're right," she admitted. "It's all... a little overwhelming."

"I'm sure it is. But you're home now."

"I'll need a car."

"You can use mine for now. We'll figure out the rest later."

That night, Justine moved through the house like it was a dream. She luxuriated in simple freedoms — walking barefoot, pouring herself a drink, lighting a candle without asking permission. Even small indulgences brought her peace: bubbles in the bath, snuggling with her pillow in bed.

Lying there, clean and safe, she whispered the word to herself again and again.

Free.

If I can just scrub off this prison filth, she thought, *Maybe I'll finally feel like myself again.*

*****

Blake pulled up in front of Justine's house the next morning and gave a quick honk. She came out smiling and hopped into the passenger seat.

When they arrived at their destination, he came around to open her door.

"It's a botanical garden," he said with a grin.

"I love flowers."

A gentle breeze stirred the air, sending dry leaves skittering across the sky as they walked toward a wooded path along the edge of the road. Branches brushed their legs, and sunlight filtered through the thick canopy above. The scent of pine and fresh earth lingered around them. Blake stopped and pointed to a patch of wild blueberries nestled among the shrubs.

"Are they safe to eat?"

"Absolutely." He popped a few into his mouth and grinned. "Try some."

Justine picked a handful, tasting the burst of tart sweetness on her tongue.

They followed the winding trail until it opened up into a sunlit field bursting with purple and white petunias. Laughing, Justine ran into the flowers, scooping a few into her arms. Blake joined her, and they collapsed into the soft bloom-covered grass. She could feel the warmth of his breath on her neck, and her body shivered in response.

"Your lips are blue from the berries," he said.

"So are yours," she replied, kissing him. The touch of his mouth made her laugh, the joy of being with him bubbling to the surface.

"What's so funny?"

"I was just thinking about the first time you came to see me at the prison. You were so shy."

Blake chuckled. "I was under a lot of pressure. Your father had just hired me to defend you—and then I looked into your eyes and knew you were the one."

He reached for the back of her neck, gently untied her halter top, and pulled her against him. She kissed him with urgency. They had known each other for months, but in prison, physical boundaries kept them apart. Now, everything they had held back surged forward.

The sound of rustling leaves snapped them out of the moment.

"Wait," she whispered, breathless.

A hiker passed nearby, unaware of them lying in the field. They stayed still until he disappeared down the path. Blake brushed her hair back and kissed her again, but she pulled away and quickly tied her top.

"What's wrong?" he asked.

"Not here," she said. "Let's go back to your place."

"You don't have to ask me twice."

Blake drove faster than usual, anxious and a little wild with anticipation, worried their passion might cool before they made it home.

At the door, he fumbled with his keys. Then, in one swift move, he scooped Justine into his arms, carried her to the bedroom, and kicked the door open with his foot.

He laid her down gently and took off his shirt. Justine watched him undress and felt the moment settle around them. This wasn't like the times before — this was real, intimate, and unguarded. She'd had sex before, but never like this. This time, she was giving more than her body. It was her heart, her mind, and a fragile hope for true love. It felt like standing at the edge of a cliff, about to leap and trust that she would fly.

Blake's kisses were full of heat but softened with care, his tongue exploring her mouth with reverence. She kissed him back, starving for connection, for something that had been denied to her for too long. His lips left hers to explore her neck, her ears, her breasts.

Justine melted into the mattress, her body one with the bed beneath her.

Blake didn't disappoint. It was astonishing how different sex felt when a man wanted more than your body.

Afterward, Justine lay curled in his arms, studying the room. Everything was in its place—neat and precise. A tray on the dresser held watches, a clothes brush, and a bottle of cologne.

"Move in with me," he said suddenly.

She hesitated. "I don't know."

He laughed softly against her skin. "We love each other. What else is there to know?"

"I've made a lot of mistakes, Blake. I don't want to mess this up."

"I get it," he said. "Let's just take it one day at a time. But tonight, you're in my arms—and that's what matters."

"Thank you," she whispered, resting her head on his chest.

They lay together as he told her about the future—his plans, his hopes. Eventually, his words drifted off as sleep claimed him.

But Justine remained awake, staring at the ceiling.

Prison had been simpler in its own strange way. It told you when to wake up, when to eat, and what to wear. There were no decisions to make, no futures to plan. Now, everything was wide open—and terrifying.

Outside, headlights swept across the wall, casting shadows that danced like ghosts.

I could move in with Blake, she thought. Part of her wanted that life. But the memory of Carl still lived inside her like a wound. That betrayal had shaken her to the core. She wasn't sure if she could ever give her full trust to a man again.

Not yet.

Freedom

The rich aroma of coffee woke Justine. For a moment, she lingered beneath the soft sheets, not quite ready to leave the warmth of Blake's bed. Eventually, she slipped out and padded barefoot through the quiet house, following the scent.

She found him on the patio, sipping espresso beneath the morning sun.

"That smells amazing," she said, stepping outside.

"Good morning, sleepyhead. I thought you'd never wake up." He kissed her, and she smiled as she savored the taste of his lips.

Justine let out a soft, nervous laugh. "I guess I'm still used to waking up to an alarm every day."

"Well, there's no roll call here, honey. You can sleep as late as you want."

"As tempting as that sounds, I feel like there's so much I want to do—and not enough daylight to do it."

"I've been up since dawn," he said, lifting the lid on a small pastry box. "Ran to the bakery and picked up some croissants."

"Oh wow, these look incredible." She picked one up and pulled it apart, admiring the delicate layers before taking a bite. It melted on her tongue—flaky, buttery perfection. "Mmm... I've missed this."

"I'll get you a cup of coffee. How do you take it?"

"Strong, with just a little cream—if you have some."

By the time Blake returned with her cup, she was already halfway through her second croissant.

"Wow. Someone's making up for lost time," he teased.

"Not really hungry," she said with a shrug. "But after everything, it's like my senses are waking up again. Good food, fresh air... It's like I'm alive for the first time."

"Would you like me to scramble some eggs?"

She made a face. "No, thanks. That's the one thing prison had plenty of—though they were always either too dry or runny enough to drink."

They both laughed.

Justine took a slow sip of her coffee, letting it swirl on her tongue before swallowing. "So... what's the plan for today?"

"I need to check on my horse. Thought maybe you'd want to come to the farm with me?"

"Oh, I'd love that."

"Great. I'll pack us a picnic—some sandwiches, maybe fruit. But I'll warn you, I may have a bit of work to do while we're there."

"I can help," she offered.

He grinned. "It's hard work."

She flexed her arm with exaggerated pride. "Look at these muscles. You think I sat around in prison all day?"

He squeezed her bicep, chuckling. "Whew. Now I know your secret — lifting weights in the yard."

They laughed together, the easy rhythm between them growing stronger with every exchange.

"Is it far?" she asked.

"Not too bad. About an hour west of here. I call it 'farmland.' Quiet, peaceful — nothing but open fields, horses, and fresh air."

Justine smiled and leaned back in her chair, croissant in one hand, coffee in the other. "I can't wait."

*****

The fall air was crisp and clean as they drove out of town that morning, though the sun was already blazing. According to the forecast, the temperature would climb into the nineties — a rare heatwave for the season.

When they arrived at the farm, Blake gave Justine a tour of the property before changing into his work clothes. She followed him to the stables, where the earthy scent of hay, horses, and dust was unfamiliar but strangely comforting. She inhaled deeply, savoring it.

"Their bedding needs to be changed," Blake said, slicing the twine on a bale of straw.

"I have to grind some hay," he added, flipping on a large machine that roared to life, drowning out conversation. Bale after bale disappeared into the grinder, the machine chewing them down into clean bedding. Golden flakes fluttered through the air like confetti.

After a few minutes, Blake pulled off his shirt, his chest and arms slick with sweat. He wiped his forehead and paused to catch his breath. Justine watched him, captivated. Desire stirred inside her. She moved to him, wrapping her arms around his waist, not caring about the dust or the sweat.

Blake slipped a hand up her thigh, and she let out a soft moan.

"I want to make love to you," he murmured.

"Now? Here in the hay?"

"I can't think of a better place to give you an orgasm."

They dropped into the soft pile of finely chopped straw beneath them. The horses looked on, ears flicking curiously. Blake pulled off her shirt and groaned at the sight of her bare breasts, then unbuttoned her jeans, his hand sliding beneath the waistband.

"Marry me," he whispered.

Her breath hitched. For a moment, everything around them faded—the scent of hay, the heat, even the horses.

She loved him. She'd known it for a while. But his words brought the weight of everything rushing back.

"Blake…" she began, her voice thick with emotion. "I love you. You know I do. But I can't—"

"Why not?" he asked, his voice tender but confused. "We've already been through so much. What's stopping us now?"

Justine looked away, then back at him. "Because there are still so many women in there. Women like me—who don't have anyone. I can't just walk away from that."

He brushed her cheek with the back of his hand. "You've done so much already. You earned your freedom. You deserve happiness. Marry me."

His lips found her neck. His hands moved across her skin. She gave in to the moment, though a sudden twinge of panic passed through her when she realized he hadn't used a condom. The thought made her flinch, but then it slipped away in the haze of his touch.

They made love again—slow and full of longing. When it was over, they lay together, drowsy and tangled in each other, until the loud neigh of a horse startled them awake.

"Mmm. I'm hungry," Blake said, stretching.

"Me too. Why don't you grab the sandwiches from the car?" Justine smiled lazily. "I'll wait here."

"Yes, your Highness." He stood, pulling on his pants but leaving his shirt and shoes behind as he headed out.

He was gone longer than she expected. Justine dressed and was about to go look for him when he returned, looking sheepish.

"You're not going to believe this... I forgot the picnic basket. It's still on the kitchen counter."

"Oh no!" She laughed. "So now what?"

"I know a great diner in town. Best burgers you've ever had."

"Burgers sound yummy."

"Then let's go."

They slid into a booth at the diner, sharing pickles from a big jar and sipping thick chocolate shakes between kisses and laughter. Their fingers kept finding each other across the table.

Blake's sky-blue eyes were thoughtful as he took a big bite of his burger. Then he slid out of his seat and joined her on her side of the booth.

"I don't like being far away from you," he said softly.

"I know. It's torture when we're apart."

He picked up a paper straw wrapper, twisted it into a ring, and slipped it onto her finger. "Let's get married."

Justine's eyes lit up. "All right."

His mouth dropped open. She giggled and popped a French fry into it.

She lifted her hand, admiring the makeshift ring. "I love it."

Blake laughed, his gaze soft. "It'll do for now. But I'd like you to wear my mother's wedding band."

"I'd be honored," she said.

Family Planning

Three months passed in a blur. Justine spent nearly every moment with Blake. While he was at work, she focused on planning their wedding.

"I want to get married on the beach," she told him one night over dinner. "After being cooped up so long, the last thing I want is a ceremony in some stuffy church."

"I want to make you happy," Blake replied. "You know what they say —' Happy wife, happy life.'"

She smiled. "We should send an invitation to your family."

His smile faltered. "That won't be necessary. My parents died in a car accident during my last year of law school."

"Oh, Blake... I'm so sorry. What about your brother, Michael? You mentioned you were close."

He looked away. "We were. But he had a falling out with our father years ago. After the accident, he just... disappeared. Left Pennsylvania without a word. No one's heard from him since."

"Have you tried to find him?"

"I did, for a long time. But I finally gave up. I don't think he wants to be found. Still... if I ever have a son, I'd like to name him after Michael."

Justine nodded. *Maybe that's why he wants a child so badly*, she thought. *To fill the space his brother left behind.*

"Well," she said gently, "I guess it won't be a big wedding—but that's okay. I have plenty of cousins, and we've got good friends. That's all we need."

"There's one other thing," Blake said. "I'm not sure when I can take time off. We might have to delay the honeymoon."

"Hmm. What about a stay-cation?"

He raised an eyebrow. "What's that?"

"It's when you check into a hotel or condo close to home. We could rent a beach house. That's where we can have the reception—and once the guests leave, it becomes our honeymoon suite."

Blake grinned. "You're brilliant. You think of everything."

"I've always been a problem solver. Sometimes it gets me into trouble, but I can't help it."

"It's one of the many things I love about you."

*****

Justine visited the church where she'd made her First Holy Communion. The priest agreed to conduct the wedding ceremony on the beach, on the condition that they have a private sacrament in the church first.

Blake didn't hide his disdain. Organized religion, in his view, was just another tool the wealthy used to control the masses. He hadn't always felt that way—he'd once been an altar boy. His mother, like Justine's, had taken the sacraments seriously. But over time, his beliefs had hardened.

Justine explained how important it was to her and gently added, "When we have children, I'd like them to receive some religious instruction."

The mention of children softened him immediately. He relented with a sigh and a kiss on her cheek. "Okay. If it means that much to you."

*****

Next on her to-do list: finding the perfect beach house. She stopped at a local real estate office and spoke with an agent.

"I've got a few options," the woman said. "But since this is for a wedding, I know just the place. A two-bedroom beach rental with a huge patio—it just came on the market."

"I'd love to see it," Justine said.

"I can show it to you now, if you'd like."

"Would it be okay if I came back tomorrow with my fiancé?"

"You could, but I can't promise it'll still be available. I've had several inquiries already this morning."

Justine hesitated, then smiled. "I guess a quick peek wouldn't hurt."

"I'm Marcy, by the way."

"Nice to meet you. I'm Justine."

They drove to the property, and when Marcy pulled into the driveway, Justine's heart skipped. The house had cheerful yellow siding that made it look like it belonged in a postcard.

Inside, the open layout took her breath away. The kitchen featured a long island with bar stools, and the living room opened up to a sliding door that led to a large back porch with an ocean view.

It was perfect.

"I'll take it," she said, and left a deposit on what the agent called the Driftwood House.

Justine was excited—but overwhelmed. She'd dreamt of her wedding since she was a little girl playing with her bridal Barbie. She'd hoped to do everything herself, but the task was starting to feel daunting.

She thought of Angie, her childhood best friend.

They had gone to high school together, roomed in the same college dorm, and lost touch only when Justine moved home. Angie still lived in Miami. Justine called her right away.

Angie was thrilled. "I'm so happy for you—and relieved you're not with that narcissist Carl anymore."

"It took prison to break free of him," Justine said. "But that's where I met Blake."

"If he treats you right, I already love him."

"He does. He wants to get married soon, so I'm trying to tie up all the details."

"I can help! Just tell me what you need."

"I missed you so much," Justine said. "It'll mean the world to have you here."

The afternoon before the wedding, Justine and Blake arrived at the beach house. She gasped as she stepped inside.

The entire space had been transformed into a bridal suite. Everything was white—walls, linens, curtains—except for pastel vases of fresh flowers on every surface. Light streamed through the sheer window panels, casting a soft glow.

"I'll grab the suitcases," Blake said.

"Great. I'll take my gown to the bedroom so it doesn't wrinkle."

She stepped into the master bedroom and found the bedspread decorated with hundreds of pink rose petals. The room was airy and romantic—just as she'd imagined it.

She unzipped the garment bag and removed her simple A-line dress, hanging it carefully. Then she placed a small satin-and-lace wedding pouch over the hanger. She gently traced the tiny flowers embroidered onto her flat bridal sandals before tucking them away again. Since they'd be standing on sand, she planned to go barefoot.

Blake called from the kitchen. He was unpacking a massive welcome basket filled with goodies—chocolates, a jar of caviar, crackers, and a chilled bottle of champagne. Two crystal flutes sat on the counter.

He popped the cork.

"To us," he said, handing her a glass.

They clinked glasses and took a sip.

Justine leaned against the counter. "Do you have any reservations?"

"Not a one," he said, his eyes warm. "I'm marrying the woman I want to be the mother of my children."

Children... Justine smiled softly as she sipped again. *There he goes again.*

Wedding

Justine was up before the sun. Blake was still snoring softly as she slipped out of bed and padded quietly into the kitchen. She started a pot of coffee, then stepped outside for a walk along the beach.

The horizon was just beginning to glow, painted in soft shades of orange and coral. As she walked barefoot in the sand, her thoughts drifted to the day ahead — and far beyond.

Will our marriage last until we're old and gray? she wondered. *Things aren't like they used to be. People start out devoted, but life has a way of creeping in — temptations, distractions...*

A group of gulls scattered at her approach, except for one. It stood its ground, fixing her with a beady, unblinking stare.

"Shoo!" she called, waving her arms.

The gull finally took flight, circled overhead, then swooped back low, taunting her. She quickened her pace, laughing under her breath, and put distance between them. The air was sweet and salty, and the rhythmic hush of waves soothed her restless mind.

No sense worrying about the future, she told herself. *Overthinking will drive me crazy.*

When she returned to the house, Blake was still asleep. She poured herself a cup of coffee from the pot — using the white mug labeled *Bride* — and stepped out onto the porch. In the distance, dark clouds hovered low over the horizon.

She narrowed her eyes. *If those clouds roll in, we might have to move everything indoors.*

"Good morning," Blake said from behind her, pulling her out of her thoughts. "Happy wedding day!"

Justine turned with a smile. "I thought you were going to sleep through it."

"I've been working nonstop. Once I fell asleep, I was out cold."

"Want some coffee?"

"I'd love some."

"Here — take mine. I'll make another cup."

He took a sip and raised an eyebrow. "How much of this did you have?"

"Enough," she laughed.

Just then, tires crunched across the gravel driveway.

"That must be Angie!" Justine said, rushing to the front of the house.

She threw her arms around her best friend. "You're amazing, Angie. Everything looks beautiful."

"I had a little help," Angie said with a smirk.

"Oh?"

"Blake. He insisted on being part of it. Sprinkling rose petals on the bed? His idea."

Justine beamed. "He's such a romantic."

"The tables and chairs should be delivered any minute," Angie continued. "Since the weather's cooperating, I figured we'd set up on the patio."

"What about the caterers? The band?"

"Don't worry, I've got it all under control. And even if they all get the flu, I have backups."

Soon after, the florist arrived with armfuls of flowers, including a stunning bridal bouquet of roses and lilies. Everything was falling into place.

"I made us appointments at the salon for hair and nails," Justine said.

Angie grinned. "No need. They're coming here."

"Seriously?"

"Seriously. Consider it my wedding gift."

At that moment, her father appeared behind them.

"Isn't it bad luck for the groom to see the bride before the wedding?" he teased.

Justine laughed and turned to kiss his cheek. "I don't believe in old superstitions, Dad."

"I guess I'm just old-fashioned," he said, his eyes twinkling. "How are you feeling, sweetheart? Nervous?"

"Actually… no." She glanced up at the sky. "As long as the rain holds off, I think it's going to be perfect."

*****

Just in case the old superstition held any truth, Justine chose to get ready in the second bedroom, leaving Blake behind in the room adorned with rose petals.

Her hair had been styled in a loose, tousled braid down her back, and her nails were freshly polished. With Angie's help, she stepped into her simple, elegant gown.

Outside, the guests had begun to arrive, their cheerful voices drifting into the house as they carried brightly wrapped gifts and cards in festive envelopes.

"I think it's time," Angie said, peeking through the curtain. "The priest is here. Blake's waiting at the trellis."

Justine took a deep breath and turned to the mirror, giving her reflection one last look.

When her father saw her step into the hallway, he brought his hands to his face, overcome. Tears welled in his eyes.

"I just wish your mother were here to see you," he whispered, wiping at his cheeks. "You're absolutely glowing."

Justine laughed gently. "No, Dad — pregnant women glow. Brides blush."

The music began, soft and sweet, and she linked her arm through his. Together, they stepped outside, greeted by smiling faces and the warm murmur of admiration.

A chorus of *oohs* and *ahhs* followed her as the crowd parted to make way. Justine scanned the guests for her secret surprise — Blake's long-lost brother — but there was no sign of him. Maybe he'd chosen not to come. She felt a flicker of disappointment but didn't let it spoil the moment. This was her and Blake's day.

Her eyes locked on Blake, standing beneath the trellis, the sea glittering behind him. He looked nervous and radiant all at once. Her heart fluttered with every note of the flute as she approached.

When she reached him, her father shook Blake's hand and placed her hand in his. The two men exchanged a nod of mutual respect, and then the priest began.

Friends and family gathered close, forming a semicircle in the sand. Even a few beachgoers paused nearby, curious to witness a wedding by the sea.

Justine and Blake stood beneath the arch covered in flowers, surrounded by the breeze, the surf, and the warmth of those they loved. They exchanged vows, their words steady and full of meaning.

When the priest finally said, "I now pronounce you husband and wife," the couple kissed for the first time as a married pair. Applause erupted, and the crowd followed them to the patio for the celebration.

Two long tables had been arranged on the spacious deck—one lined with crystal urns of deep red wine and champagne bottles resting in ice, the other with platters of seafood: steamed crab legs, shrimp in lemon garlic sauce, pompano grilled to perfection, and towers of lobster dumplings and caviar. Adults gathered around the delicacies while children gravitated to the mini grilled cheese sandwiches and eyed the dessert table with wide-eyed anticipation.

Justine paused, watching a flock of seagulls circling nearby. Their shrill cries made her uneasy. *Please don't swoop in on the food,* she silently begged.

After dinner, the band picked up the tempo. The mellow dinner music gave way to festive tunes, and guests kicked off their sandals to dance in the sand.

Blake took particular joy in playing with the children, letting them tag him and chase him across the beach. Laughter filled the air as he dropped to the ground, letting them bury him in sand.

"Help!" he cried out dramatically.

"You're on your own," Justine called, laughing from the patio.

She watched him, her heart full. *He's going to be a good father,* she thought. *Kind. Patient. Fun.*

Still, the thought of raising children made her nervous. Would she be a good mother? She didn't know. The uncertainty settled somewhere deep in her chest.

A moment later, the dessert cart rolled out to a chorus of cheers. The children raced back to the patio at the sight of the wedding cake, a towering white confection decorated with seashells and sugared flowers.

Blake stood and brushed the sand from his clothes, joining Justine at the front of the gathering.

"Thank you all for coming," he said, raising his glass. "Justine and I are so grateful to be surrounded by so much love today. This isn't just a wedding celebration—it's a reunion. A chance to be with familiar faces and welcome new ones into our lives."

The crowd clapped, and Justine raised her glass alongside him, her smile wide, her heart full.

Surprise Guest

The wedding was in full swing when Blake noticed a tall, thin man in a blue shirt and jeans stepping out of the house.

He froze, squinting. Then his fork clattered to the table as he jumped to his feet.

"Michael!" he shouted, rushing over. "Michael — is it really you?"

Blake pulled his brother into a bear hug, holding on tightly as if afraid he might vanish.

"How did you find me?"

"Your lovely wife tracked me down," Michael said, smiling.

Justine joined them. "I'm really glad you came. Honestly, I wasn't sure you would."

"Sorry, I'm late. I got stuck in traffic on Okeechobee Boulevard. And I'm not exactly familiar with the East Coast."

"Wait — you live in Florida?"

"Yeah. Clearwater."

Blake's jaw dropped. "You mean all this time you've been practically under my nose, and I didn't know it? I thought you'd moved out west — you always talked about California."

Michael shrugged. "I had a lot of issues to work through. I'm sorry I haven't been in touch."

Blake shook his head, overwhelmed. "It doesn't matter. You're here now. That's what counts. How long can you stay?"

"Just the day, I'm afraid. I have to get back to work tomorrow."

"Where are you staying?"

"I booked a hotel in town."

Blake looked disappointed. "You should've stayed with us."

Michael laughed. "On your honeymoon? I think three's a crowd. Besides, I'm sure your bride wants you all to herself."

Blake started to respond, but Michael cut him off. "Don't worry. I'll come back — with my family."

Blake's eyes lit up. "Family?"

"I'm married now. Three beautiful daughters."

Justine beamed. "Why didn't you bring them?"

"I thought it best to come alone," Michael admitted. "It's been so long since we saw each other. I didn't want to overwhelm you."

Blake's voice was thick with emotion. "I'm overwhelmed in the best possible way. This... this is the greatest wedding gift I could've asked for." He turned and hugged Justine. "I married an incredible woman."

"You sure did," Michael said, grinning. "You did good, Blake."

"I found my soulmate."

"Come sit with us," Blake said. "I want to hear everything. You're my brother, but you're also a stranger."

"Yes," Justine chimed in. "We'd love for you to join us."

"I'd be honored."

Michael took a seat at their table and lifted his glass. The other guests quickly followed his lead.

"I propose a toast," he said, raising his voice. "To the lovely couple — may they have an eternity of bliss."

"Hear, hear!" the crowd echoed in unison.

Just as the cheers faded, a sudden flurry of wings erupted above them. A flock of seagulls swooped down toward the tables.

Justine gasped as the feathered invaders snatched morsels of wedding cake. One particularly bold gull landed right on the table, its beady eyes locked on a succulent crab claw.

Justine stared in disbelief. "It's him," she muttered. "It's the same one from this morning."

She flailed her arms. "Shoo! Go on, get out of here!"

The gull squawked in protest before lifting off. The others followed, soaring back into the sky, leaving behind only crumbs — and a table full of laughter.

Guests wiped tears of mirth from their eyes. Even the children clapped and cheered.

"Well," Blake said, catching his breath. "I guess the seagulls approve of the menu."

"And the marriage," Justine added, still laughing. "Let's hope they don't crash the honeymoon."

*****

The day was winding down. After a spectacular display of color, the sun dipped below the horizon, casting a golden glow over the beach. One by one, the guests offered their final congratulations before heading off into the twilight.

Before leaving, Michael pulled Blake aside. "You two should come visit us in Clearwater," he said. "My girls would love to meet their uncle."

"We'd love that," Blake replied, giving his brother one last embrace. "Don't be a stranger this time."

Justine waved from the porch. "Thank you for coming, Michael. It meant so much to Blake—and to me."

"Thank your wife for tracking me down," he said, smiling warmly.

As Michael drove off, Angie lingered behind, taking one last look at the decorated patio.

"Don't worry about the cleanup," she said. "I arranged for someone to come tomorrow and tidy up."

Justine hugged her. "You're the best. Thank you, Angie. For everything."

"That's what friends are for," she replied, then gave a playful wink before getting in her car and heading off.

Blake slipped his arm around Justine's waist as they stood watching the taillights fade into the distance.

"So," he said, his voice low and teasing, "how does it feel to be Mrs. Sullivan?"

Justine smiled, leaning into him. "It feels just right. I don't have a single complaint. The wedding was everything I hoped it would be."

Blake pulled her close, his hands finding the tiny buttons at the back of her gown. As he undid them, he trailed soft kisses down her spine to the small of her back.

She shivered, laughing breathlessly. "I'd like to freshen up."

She slipped away with the negligee she'd bought as part of her bridal trousseau, disappearing into the bathroom.

"Okay," Blake called after her, "but don't take too long."

He popped the cork on a bottle of champagne, poured two glasses, lit a single candle, and dimmed the lights.

When Justine stepped out, he turned — and his breath caught.

"Justine…" he murmured. "You look beautiful."

She came to him slowly, smiling, the candlelight flickering over her skin. He pulled her close, kissed the nape of her neck, and wrapped his arms around her.

She could feel his heart pounding against her chest. His hands moved over her body with reverence, his touch sparking shivers across her skin. Her breath quickened. She wanted to please him — needed to feel desired, safe, and whole.

"Let's make a baby," he whispered into her ear.

Her body stilled. "A baby?"

"Why not?" he asked softly. "Let's start our family."

She pulled back slightly, searching his face. "Blake... we can't do that. Not yet."

"Why not?"

"Because we wouldn't have the time to give a child what they deserve. I haven't given up the idea of a career—and I've only just started to get my life back. We need time... to grow into ourselves first."

He nodded slowly, accepting it. "It wouldn't be so bad."

"Not for you," she said gently. "But for me, it would be everything. I'm not ready—not yet. But I know you'll be a wonderful father... when the time is right."

She kissed him again, pressing closer, grounding them in the moment.

"All right, then," he whispered, smiling against her lips. "No babies. Just fooling around."

Outside, the tide lapped rhythmically against the shore. Wrapped in each other's arms, the newlyweds drifted off to sleep, lulled by the waves—and the quiet promise of the life they were beginning together.

Brotherly Love

The morning air was cool and sweet, carrying the scent of salt and sea grass. Blake and Justine walked hand in hand along the shoreline, their footprints trailing behind them in the damp sand. Waves lapped gently at their feet, and gulls called in the distance. Neither of them spoke — they didn't need to. Their silence was filled with quiet contentment.

When the weekend drew to a close, they reluctantly said goodbye to their honeymoon suite, promising to return each year on their anniversary.

Back at the house, Blake swept Justine into his arms and carried her over the threshold — bridal style — while awkwardly trying to balance the small box holding the top layer of their wedding cake.

"Careful," Justine warned, laughing. But the box slipped from his grasp and hit the floor with a soft thud.

They brought it to the kitchen and peeled back the lid to assess the damage. The fluffy white frosting had smeared across the inside, exposing swirls of rich chocolate cake beneath.

"Well, so much for freezing it until our first anniversary," she sighed.

Blake dipped his finger into the mess and scooped up a dollop of icing. "I'm starving," he said, licking it off. "I barely got a bite of breakfast this morning."

"Neither did I."

They looked at each other, then back at the ruined cake. Without another word, they ripped the box open and began feeding each other chunks of frosting and cake with their fingers, giggling like children.

When their hunger for food was finally satisfied, their lips met—sweet and sticky with sugar and chocolate. The taste only deepened their kisses, igniting the same spark that had followed them from the beach to the bedroom.

Desire flared between them again, and the kitchen melted away as they gave in to one more indulgence—each other.

*****

Blake managed to rearrange a few of his law cases so he and Justine could visit his brother in Clearwater.

Michael's wife, Zoeie, was delightful—warm, down-to-earth, and funny. She and Justine hit it off instantly, laughing together in the kitchen as they prepared Sunday dinner while the brothers sat on the back porch, beers in hand.

"Let's take a walk," Blake said. "I have so many questions. Starting with—why did you leave?"

Michael sighed and stared out at the horizon. "I don't even know where to start. I guess it all goes back to when we were kids. Dad was hard on me. You were the golden child. I couldn't do anything right in his eyes, and after a while... I stopped trying. I guess I resented you for it, even though it wasn't your fault."

Blake frowned. "I had no idea you felt that way. If I had known... I would've tried to make it better. I should've been more aware."

"It's not on you," Michael said, shaking his head. "After Dad died, it felt like the floor dropped out. I was angry — confused. I needed space, so I ran. It's not an excuse," he added quickly. "It's just the truth."

"I wish you would've confided in me."

"There wasn't much you could've done," Michael said with a shrug. "You had your own grief."

"I blamed myself. I thought maybe I failed you somehow — as a brother."

Michael smiled and gave him a playful punch on the arm. "Nah. You were all right."

Blake chuckled. "Thanks."

Michael looked away, his voice softer. "I've had so much time to think over the years. I wanted to find you — but after how things ended, I didn't think you'd want to hear from me. You were so upset when our parents died... I figured you hated me."

"I could never hate you," Blake said. "You're my brother."

Suddenly, Michael burst into laughter — sharp and unexpected. "Sorry," he gasped. "None of this is funny. I just—God, I wasted so much time. How can you forgive me?"

Blake let out a laugh of his own. "How could I not? You're family."

From the porch, Zoeie and Justine called to them. "Dinner's ready!"

They walked back inside, the tension between them finally starting to ease.

"You know," Justine said as they sat around the table, "you should move to the East Coast. We'd love to spend more time with you and the girls."

"Funny you should say that," Michael said. "We've been thinking the same thing. I was just laid off a few weeks ago."

"I'm sorry to hear that," Justine said. "What kind of work do you do?"

"I'm in finance. Budgets, forecasts, spreadsheets—nothing thrilling."

Blake perked up. "Actually, I could use someone like you. I've been needing help on the business side of my firm."

"You're serious?"

"Absolutely. Think about it."

"I think it's a wonderful idea," Zoeie chimed in, beaming.

Blake raised his glass. "To *famiglia*—old bonds, new beginnings."

Glasses clinked, laughter rang through the dining room, and the scent of baked pasta and roasted vegetables filled the air as their long-awaited reunion turned into something even greater—a second chance.

Time

Justine had put the prison behind her in the six months since she and Blake were married. Lost in thought, she rinsed dishes in a sink full of soapy water, unaware that Blake had entered the kitchen.

He crept up behind her and wrapped his arms around her waist.

She jumped, hand to her heart. "Don't sneak up on me like that!"

"I couldn't help myself," he whispered, pressing himself against her. "You look beautiful from behind."

Justine smacked him with the dish towel. "You stop that, or you're not going to work today."

"I'd love nothing more than to drag you back into the bedroom," he teased, "but I've got a packed schedule."

"I want to help. Can't I work with you?"

His playful grin faded. "Actually, there's something I need to tell you."

Her face fell. "What is it? Is something wrong?"

Blake hesitated. "Yes... and no. I know how much you want to get back to work, but before you can practice law here, you have to pass the state's admissions process — character and fitness included."

"I'm working on it." Justine's voice trembled. "You have to help me."

"I will. But I'm a civil rights attorney. You need a criminal lawyer who understands the nuances of post-conviction admissions."

She took a shaky breath. "This isn't about the baby, is it? You're not stalling because you want to start a family?"

"No. This isn't about that. I tried to bring you on as a legal consultant, but my partner shut it down."

He handed her a business card. "This guy might be able to help. We went to college together."

Justine's cheeks flushed with frustration. "I need air," she muttered, grabbing her purse and slamming the door behind her.

She walked two miles to her father's house, her thoughts spiraling. She knew it wasn't Blake's fault — Florida's Bar wasn't friendly to applicants with a felony on their record, even one overturned.

Her father wasn't home. She stood in the hallway, staring at the framed photograph of her mother.

"What am I going to do, Mamma?" she whispered.

The front door creaked open behind her.

"Justine?" Benjamin's voice startled her. "You okay? What are you doing here?"

"Oh, Daddy…" She ran into his arms, sobbing. "I thought getting out of prison would mean a fresh start. But I still feel like a convict."

He rocked her gently. "Nonsense. It just takes time."

"I don't have time. Blake wants to start a family, and I'm not ready. I'm scared. What if I miscarry again? And I still want to be a lawyer. Maybe… maybe I made a mistake marrying him."

"Do you love him?"

"Yes," she admitted. "But what if I can't make him happy?"

She remembered how safe she felt with Blake from the start—his honeyed voice, his calm demeanor. But marriage wasn't as easy as the fairytales made it seem.

"Marriage is compromise," her father said. "You need to talk to him. Really talk. I'm sure he'll understand."

Justine nodded, wiping her eyes. "You're right. I acted like a child." She rushed home, regretting how she'd walked out. But when she got back, Blake had already gone to the office. Her anger had cooled, replaced by shame.

She called his cell. It went to voicemail.

After sitting in silence for a long while, she pulled herself together and dialed the number on the card Blake had given her.

"I'd like to speak with Mr. Beddie," she told the receptionist.

"May I ask who's calling?"

"My name is Justine. My husband is Blake Sullivan — he said they were friends."

"Hold on, please."

A moment later, a man's voice came on the line. "Hello! My receptionist says a blast from the past is on the phone."

"Well, kind of. I'm Justine — Blake's wife."

"Blake Sullivan, married?" he laughed. "Didn't think I'd live to see the day. How's he doing?"

"He's great. We live in Florida. He said you might be able to help me."

"What's going on?"

"I earned my law degree before being wrongfully convicted. I've since been released, but the Bar exam process — especially the character and fitness part — is a problem. I need advice."

Beddie's tone grew more serious. "Unfortunately, any arrest record, even overturned, tends to stick in the system. In Florida, that can create serious hurdles. Expungement takes time."

"I don't have time. I need to work now."

"Florida's tough. But not all states are. If you're open to relocating — "

"No. I can't do that to Blake."

"Then your best shot is to file a petition. It's not easy, but it's possible. I recall a similar case. The applicant won. I'll dig up the details and get back to you."

"Thank you. Blake said you were the best."

He laughed. "Tell him he still owes me a beer for that college football bet."

"I will. Thanks again."

Justine hung up. It wasn't much, but it was hope. She poured herself a glass of wine and stepped onto the porch. *Who am I kidding? I'm chasing a dream that may never be real.*

Later, she decided to shake off her despair. It was their six-month anniversary. If Blake was stressed, she'd meet him with love — not resentment. She bought veal for his favorite dinner, picked up his favorite wine, and even made ricotta tarts for dessert. The kitchen was a floury mess, but she didn't care.

The phone rang. She answered with sticky fingers. "Hello?"

"Hi, Mrs. Sullivan? I'm Blake's new paralegal. He wanted me to let you know he'll be working late."

Her heart sank. *Of course he is.*

She wrapped his plate in plastic and left it on the stove. Then she took her own meal — and the wine — into the living room.

Blake got home late. He looked exhausted.

"I'm sorry," he said. "I'm buried in this case. But when it's over, we'll go somewhere. Just us. I promise."

"That's what you said last month," she said softly. "But there's always another case, Blake."

*****

Blake was already gone when Justine woke up the next morning. The house felt too quiet, too still. She wandered into the kitchen, poured herself a cup of coffee, and stood by the window, watching the sun creep over the horizon.

Outside, her neighbor Cindy jogged past in sleek workout clothes, her ponytail bouncing with each stride. Justine followed her with her eyes until she disappeared around the corner. A flicker of something stirred in her chest—nostalgia, maybe. Back in her freshman year, she used to love running. It made her feel free, strong, and in control of her body and mind.

Maybe it was time to feel that way again.

After a long shower, she dressed and waited for the stores to open.

Using Blake's credit card, she hit the shops with a purpose. She bought yoga pants, two pairs of running shoes, and three coordinated jogging outfits. On a whim, she stopped by Radio Shack and picked up a cassette player and headset. There was something comforting about the old-school feel of it—like returning to a forgotten part of herself.

That evening, when Blake walked in, his briefcase still in hand, he raised an eyebrow at the bags and boxes cluttering the living room.

"What's all this?" he asked, dropping his keys in the bowl by the door.

Justine turned, smiling. "I've decided to take up running again."

Tent City

Indian summer held winter at bay a little longer. Justine welcomed the brisk air that kissed her cheeks as she stepped onto the street. She double-knotted the laces of her new sneakers and took off under a cloudless blue sky.

At first, she could barely run four blocks without her chest burning. She read in a magazine that increasing lung capacity took time. After two weeks, she managed three steady miles. Her breath fell into rhythm — inhale through the nose, exhale through the mouth — as her feet pounded the pavement, scattering leaves like brittle confetti. The cicadas buzzed faintly, as if even they were losing faith in the season's warmth.

She jogged past Pine Street, where the town's elite lived in sprawling estates, their driveways lined with trimmed hedges and flags declaring *God Bless America*. But as she veered closer to the park, the landscape changed. Lawns turned patchy. The scent of burnt grass lingered from the long drought. A tent city had risen from the cracks of poverty like weeds through pavement—tarp-covered, tattered, and heartbreakingly human.

Her pace slowed. The contrast jarred her—the manicured wealth behind her, and this... all too close to a life she had once known.

Then she saw her.

A woman stood near the curb, hair like steel wool, a cardboard sign strung around her neck: *Hungry. Need Food.* Their eyes locked.

Justine skidded to a stop, her breath catching. Her pulse drummed in her ears. "Sara?"

The woman flinched. "I don't have friends," she said, her voice dry and bitter.

"It's me—Justine. From Danbury."

Sara's gaze was guarded. "That was a long time ago."

"I didn't know you were out. What happened?"

"What didn't?" she snapped. "You said you'd help me when I got out. But you disappeared. I guess once you got your life back, I wasn't worth remembering."

"That's not true."

"I learned from you. Watched how you said the right things, kept your head down. I did the same. Got paroled. Thought maybe I had a shot."

Justine softened. "Then what?"

"My ex. He sabotaged everything. Jobs, apartments... even my chance to see my kids. Told the court I was using again."

"And are you?"

Sara laughed without humor. "Would it even matter if I said no?"

"It matters to me."

"Hope is a cruel trick, Justine. You start to believe again, and it yanks the rug out from under you."

Justine looked at the broken woman, so different from the sharp-witted friend she once knew — but not beyond saving. "Come home with me. Just until you get back on your feet."

"Really?"

"We've got space. Blake won't mind."

Sara hesitated, then glanced back at her makeshift life stuffed in plastic bags. "This is all I have."

"Then we'll bring it too."

Back at the house, Sara stood in awe beneath the arched entry, eyeing the antique armoire. "This yours?"

"Blake's. It's been in his family for generations."

"I bet it's worth more than everything I've ever owned."

Justine offered a tight smile. The air had thickened with the scent of sweat and city grime. She glanced at the clock. Blake would be home soon — she had to move fast.

"I'll show you to the guest room. There's a private bath. Take as long as you need."

In the bathroom, steam curled from the shower as Sara stepped in. The water washed over her, peeling away layers of exhaustion and shame. She scrubbed until her skin stung. When she emerged, she found clean clothes folded on the bed and a comforter that smelled of jasmine. She sank into it, barely registering the silk beneath her fingers before sleep claimed her.

She woke to voices.

"She's here? In our house?" Blake asked, stunned.

Justine's voice was soft, but firm. "Yes. She was living in the tent city. I couldn't leave her there."

"She could be using. You can't save everyone."

"I'm not trying to save everyone. Just her."

From the hallway, Sara stepped into view. Her voice was quiet, but steady. "Hi. I'm Sara."

Blake turned. He took her outstretched hand — but his gaze flicked to the faint marks on her arm. Something hardened in his expression. The warmth he usually carried dimmed.

Justine saw it. Felt it. And for the first time since Sara stepped into their home, a pit opened in her stomach.

What had she done?

Thief

The next morning, Justine called the county clerk's office and asked to speak with Commissioner Howard.

"I'll take a message," the receptionist said. "He'll call when he's free."

Justine left her number. Then she called again. And again. By the fifth call, she didn't bother with politeness.

"Tell him I won't stop until I speak with him. It's urgent."

An hour later, her phone finally rang.

"Hello?"

"Is this Justine Morgan?" a clipped voice asked.

"Yes."

"This is Commissioner Howard. I understand you have an urgent matter."

"Thank you for calling. I'm calling about the women in Tent City."

"We're doing everything we can to get rid of them, I assure you."

"No! That's not what I meant—"

"Then what *do* you mean?" His tone was sharp.

"I'm asking the county to help them. Provide real shelter. A path forward."

"You assume they *want* homes? Some prefer living outside. It's a lifestyle choice for them."

"No, not all. Many don't have a choice. They need safe housing, not sidewalks and benches."

"There are low-income units. They just need jobs."

Justine's voice tightened. "It's not that simple. Many have children and no childcare. Some were incarcerated and cannot pass a background check. They *want* to work, but they're blocked at every turn."

"And you think a free house will fix that?"

"If we help even one woman escape poverty, her children benefit. And their children after them. That's how you rebuild a community."

"I'm late for another meeting," he said abruptly. "Best of luck."

The line went dead.

Justine stared at the phone. Her hands trembled with frustration. But she wasn't done. There was another commissioner she remembered from a news segment—a woman known for taking action.

Commissioner Laura Mosely.

Justine drove to the government offices. The same receptionist sat at the front desk.

"Can I help you?"

"I'd like to speak with Commissioner Mosely."

"She's not seeing visitors today."

"This can't wait."

"I'll leave a note on her desk."

Justine turned to leave — then spun back and strode past the desk.

"Wait — you can't go in there!" the receptionist called, rushing after her.

But Justine had already knocked.

Commissioner Mosely looked up, startled but composed.

"I'm sorry, Commissioner," the receptionist said breathlessly. "She — "

"It's fine," Mosely said. "You've got sixty seconds. What's this about?"

"The homeless women at Tent City," Justine said. "They need homes, not citations and jail time."

"We're working to clean it up. That camp is a health hazard — typhoid, hepatitis, God knows what else."

"And pushing them out only spreads the problem. We need permanent solutions, not punishment."

"There are shelters — two in this county alone."

"Which kicks them out after ninety days. Then what? There's a shortage of affordable housing, and landlords won't rent to anyone with a record."

Mosely sighed. "You're preaching to the choir. I've been fighting for affordable housing since I was elected. But funding is tight, and the public wants results, not handouts."

"What about *Housing First*?"

Mosely tilted her head. "I've read about it. California's pilot program?"

"It worked. L.A. cut homelessness by more than half with a voucher system and anti-discrimination laws. Utah dropped homelessness by *ninety percent* when they adopted it."

The commissioner leaned back in her chair and tapped her pen. "You think our governor would sign something like that?"

"If it's proposed in the right way — maybe."

"And then it would go to the legislature."

"If they veto it?"

"Then it advances to the House and Senate."

"And if they stall?"

She smiled. "Then Housing First becomes law by default."

Justine felt a jolt of hope.

"I'll draft a proposal," Mosely said. "You'll need to help build community support. I can't do this alone."

"I'll do whatever it takes."

For the first time all day, Justine allowed herself to believe something might change. Not tomorrow. Not easily. But soon.

And maybe this time, *she* could be the one making the difference.

*****

For the second week in a row, temperatures hovered below freezing. Justine jogged on the treadmill in the basement, the rhythmic thump of her feet echoing off the cement walls. She hated the windowless room — it felt like a bunker — but the icy wind outside left her no choice.

Running used to clear her head. Lately, it just exhausted her.

Upstairs, rain battered the windows, and wind howled against the front door like some restless spirit clawing to get inside. A hurricane watch was in effect.

Justine poured two glasses of red wine and returned to the living room, where she and Sara sat across from each other with a game of chess between them.

"The storm's moving in," Sara said, peering out the window. "Wind's howlin' like a ghost looking for a way in."

Justine stood and pressed her face to the glass. The yard was a blur of shadows and shivering branches. "I wonder how they're holding up at Tent City."

Sara leaned back. "You think Blake's gonna make it home tonight?"

"It depends. If the roads get too bad, he might sleep at the office. He's done it before."

Sara stayed through the winter and into the spring. She tried holding jobs, but never lasted more than a few days. She overslept, left early, and called in sick more than she showed up.

One night, as Justine cleared the dinner dishes, Blake pulled her aside. "When is this girl going to leave?"

"She has no place to go," Justine said. "I'm not going to throw her out into the street."

Blake exhaled through his nose. "It's not that I don't like her. It's just..." He hesitated, then shook his head. "I don't know. Something feels off. I can't put my finger on it."

Justine crossed her arms. "Is this about the wine? The food? The laundry?"

"No," he said quietly. "It's not that. It's her energy. The way she watches everything. Like she's casing the place."

"Don't be ridiculous," Justine said, though a chill crawled up her spine.

Blake hunched his shoulders helplessly. "Never mind."

But the doubt lingered, floating unspoken between them, as ominous as the storm pounding at their door.

*****

The house was still.

Sara peeked out the front window. Justine's car was gone. She was finally alone.

Moving quietly, she crept down the hallway and turned the knob to the master bedroom. Unlocked. She slipped inside and flicked on the light.

The room smelled faintly of lavender. Two tidy racks filled the closet—Justine's skirts and blouses on one side, Blake's dress shirts and suits on the other. His shoes were lined up in precise rows. Justine's were jumbled in a heap.

Nothing worth taking.

She shut the closet door and turned to the dresser. Her eyes lit on the velvet jewelry box perched on top. With trembling fingers, she lifted the lid.

Gold chains. A string of pearls. A few rings. One caught the light just right—a square-cut diamond surrounded by tiny sapphires. She picked it up and turned it over, admiring how it sparkled. Without thinking, she slid it into her pocket.

"What are you doing?"

Sara froze.

Justine stood in the doorway, arms folded, voice like ice.

"I—I was just looking," Sara stammered.

"In my jewelry box?"

Sara's breath caught in her throat. "I wasn't going to take anything."

"I saw you." Justine's voice cracked. "You put something in your pocket."

Sara's face drained of color. She began to hyperventilate. "Please... I—"

"You're a thief," Justine said flatly. "Blake was right about you."

"No. I swear, I've never stolen anything before."

"Then why me, Sara?" Her voice trembled now, more hurt than angry. "I trusted you."

"I can't—" Sara's voice broke. "I can't tell you."

Justine stepped forward, her expression hardening. "Tell me, or you're out of this house."

Sara collapsed to the floor, body shaking. "I'm an addict," she whispered. "I need it. I—I didn't want to go back to using, but I couldn't help it."

Justine's heart sank. "How long?"

"Since Tent City. Someone gave me heroin. I thought it would take the pain away. I was wrong."

"How have you been paying for it?"

Sara looked away. "I held a cardboard sign that said *hungry*. People gave me money."

Justine felt sick. "If Blake finds out…"

"Please," Sara begged, gripping her knees. "Don't tell him. I'll stop. I swear, I'll get clean."

"You *want* to stop," Justine said. "But that's not enough. You need help."

"I'll go anywhere. You can take me. Just don't give up on me."

Justine studied her. A moment passed, heavy and quiet. Then she nodded.

"Okay. We'll find a program. But if you relapse here, you're gone."

Sara let out a shaky breath. "Thank you. I don't know where I'd be without you."

Justine extended her hand. "Give me the ring."

Sara reached into her pocket and held it out, eyes downcast. "I'm sorry."

Justine took it gently and closed the box. Neither of them spoke. The silence was heavy with shame… and the flicker of something that might still be hope.

Reckoning

Justine still felt the weight of guilt for losing touch with her prison friends. Thoughts of Fran surfaced — her sharp humor, her quiet resilience. She dug through her desk drawer until she found the last letter Fran had written. Scrawled at the bottom was a phone number and address. Without hesitation, she dialed.

Fran answered on the second ring, her voice lighting up with surprise and joy. "Justine? No way!"

They agreed to meet at a small diner near Fran's job. She only had an hour lunch break, but insisted on squeezing it in.

At noon, Justine rushed inside, brushing rain from her coat. Fran spotted her from a corner booth and waved.

"I'm so sorry I'm late," Justine said, sliding into the seat across from her. "There was an accident. Traffic was at a standstill."

Fran grinned. "No problem. I'll just get a doggie bag. Woof, woof."

They both laughed and embraced across the table.

"It's so good to see you," Justine said. "You look amazing."

"Yeah, well, freedom suits me better than orange jumpsuits and hairnets. Who'd have thought we'd be here—two ex-cons eating something that didn't come from a can."

Justine chuckled. "So... how's everything going? Any progress with your daughter?"

Fran's smile faltered. "Trying. Family court's a slow crawl through hell. I have to show proof of stable housing first, and the halfway house I'm in now is shutting down."

"I heard that was happening. I'm so sorry."

"I've looked into everything. Section 8 sounds great—on paper. But the waitlist is ridiculous. Over a year, maybe longer. I filled out every form, went to all the classes, but that doesn't change the math. There are more applicants than homes."

"You've done everything right, Fran."

"It doesn't feel like it. My caseworker's doing what she can, but with a court-appointed attorney? Family court chews people like me up and spits them out. It's humiliating. I feel like I'm being punished just for wanting my child back."

Justine reached across the table and squeezed her hand. "You *are* a good mother. The system's broken, not you. It kills me how many men weaponize the courts to destroy the women who raised their children—all for money or pride. And the kids are the ones who suffer most."

Fran gave a bitter laugh. "These guys don't even want to be fathers. They just want to win. And the courts let it happen."

Justine took a breath. "I told Blake about your case."

"You did?"

"He wants to help. He said he'll represent you."

Fran's mouth opened in disbelief. "Justine... I can't afford him."

"You don't have to. He said he'll take the case pro bono. He does it all the time for people who've been denied a fair shot just because they can't afford real legal help."

Tears welled in Fran's eyes, but she blinked them back. "You think he can really help me?"

"I know he can. I'll check his schedule and set up a time for the two of you to meet. I'll come with you if you want."

Fran nodded slowly, her voice thick. "That would mean the world to me."

Justine smiled. "But enough doom and gloom. I'm starving. I hear this place has the best burgers in town."

Fran grinned. "Now you're speaking my language."

*****

On her way home, Justine slowed as she passed the halfway house. Its tired brick façade seemed to sag under the weight of all the women who had passed through it, trying to rebuild their lives with nothing. Righteous anger surged through her veins—not just for Fran, but for all the women she had left behind. They deserved more than bunk beds and ticking clocks on institutional walls. *If only I could buy the place,* she thought. Then, almost on cue, a different image came to her—a large house she'd seen listed for sale weeks ago.

Curious, she swung by the neighborhood.

The "Open House" sign was still posted on the lawn like a beacon. Her heart skipped. *It hasn't sold yet?* She parked at the curb and stepped out, her pulse quickening.

Inside, a young couple was already touring the house. The wife frowned at the outdated kitchen tile, while the husband tried to sell her on the potential. The real estate agent, a cheerful woman with beachy blonde waves and a skirt too short for winter, was doing her best to win them over.

Justine wandered through the first floor. Four bedrooms—five if she counted the finished basement. A kitchen with ample cabinetry. An open dining area big enough to hold a long farmhouse table. The walls could use a fresh coat of paint, but the bones of the place were solid. *Functional. Safe. Hopeful.*

She wanted it. Needed it.

When the couple left, the agent approached with a wide smile. "Hi, I'm Sandy. Are you interested in the house?"

"Yes," Justine said. "It's perfect."

"For just you?" Sandy glanced at her modest outfit and running shoes.

"No. I want to open a transitional home for women released from prison. A safe place to start over."

The agent's smile dimmed slightly. "Oh. Well... the down payment is rather significant."

"How much?"

"The seller's asking price is two twenty-five. You'd need ten percent to hold the offer — twenty-two five."

Justine smiled. "I'll call my broker. I'll see how much stock I can liquidate."

Sandy's expression faltered. "It's a competitive market. This house won't last long."

It's been sitting here for two months, Justine thought. *Don't lie to me.*

On her way home, she stopped by her father's house. He sat on the porch in his usual spot, puffing on a cigar, the smoke curling into the air like old thoughts.

"I hope you haven't given up on the Bar exam," Benjamin said. "You worked too hard for that law degree. It would be a shame to waste it."

"I haven't forgotten. But I need a favor."

He arched a brow.

"Can I borrow eighteen-five from my trust?"

"What for?"

"I want to buy a house. Not for me — for them. The women who have nowhere to go after release. There's a property in town. Huge, clean, safe. I want to turn it into a home."

His expression darkened with concern. "And how will you pay the mortgage?"

"I'm starting a nonprofit. Filing for 501(c)(3) status. I'll apply for subsidies. Blake set me up with a firm that needs payroll services—reliable work I can do from home. I plan to hire the residents. We'll build the business together. All I need is the deposit to start."

He scratched his temple and puffed on the cigar. "I don't think there's much left in that account."

"Can you check?"

"I will. First thing tomorrow. But don't get your hopes up. Law school drained most of it."

Justine kissed him on the cheek. "Thanks, Dad."

Back at home, she gathered the mail from the floor and dropped her keys in the bowl. The microwave's digital clock blinked *4:30 p.m.*, still off from the last power outage. Her phone read *5:30*. Blake had promised to be home by six. He usually kept that promise.

She poured a glass of water and sat at the kitchen table. A name surfaced in her thoughts—Marc Mauer. She had met him at a dinner party months ago. He and Blake had worked together on reform issues. Marc was the executive director of the Sentencing Project. If anyone could help her break through the red tape of the Bar Association, it was him.

Even if he mostly worked on behalf of male offenders, Justine knew she had to try.

She picked up the phone and dialed his number.

*****

Blake watched, amused, as Justine spooned sugar — one, two, three, four heaping scoops—into her coffee.

"Wow," he said. "You planning to run a marathon before noon?"

"I need the energy. Yesterday was rough. I feel like I'm on a losing streak."

"You can't give up." He rinsed his cup and leaned down to kiss the top of her head. "Something will turn around. It always does. I'll try to make it home early tonight."

She gave a tired laugh. "Don't worry. I'll keep your dinner warm — again."

The door clicked shut behind him. A second later, the phone rang.

"I have good news," Benjamin's voice boomed through the line.

Justine straightened. "What is it?"

"There's fifteen thousand left in your trust."

She sighed. "But that's not enough. I need at least twenty-two. That's still seven grand short."

"I'll cover the rest."

"What?" Her voice cracked. "Dad, you don't have to do that."

"I know. I want to. Justine, I can't take it with me, and I'd rather see that money do something meaningful now — something that matters to you."

A soft laugh escaped her. "What did I ever do to deserve such a great father?"

"You were born. That was enough. If I can't support my daughter in her biggest endeavor yet, then I've failed as a father."

"I love you, Dad." Her voice wavered. "I'm sorry I turned out to be such a disappointment."

"Don't you *ever* say that again." His voice turned firm. "You have never disappointed me. If anything,

I've been hard on myself for not protecting you from everything that happened. All I've ever wanted was your happiness."

"I *am* happy. I just wish Mom were here to see it."

"She is. She's smiling down on you from heaven, proud of the woman you've become."

Justine wiped her eyes with her sleeve. "I just want to change lives. You're making that possible."

"I'll wire the money into your account this morning. It should be there before noon."

"Thank you, Dad."

As promised, the funds hit her account by 11:45 a.m. She wasted no time. She drove straight to the house, the check clutched tightly in her hand, her stomach fluttering with excitement.

The real estate agent greeted her with a polite smile, but Justine noticed it didn't reach her eyes.

"I have the money," she said, breathless. She held up the check like it was a golden ticket.

Sandy hesitated. "Oh, Justine… I'm so sorry. The house is no longer available. It went under contract this morning."

Her heart dropped. "You mean—someone bought it?"

"Yes. The couple from the open house submitted a bid yesterday evening. The seller accepted it this morning."

Justine stood in stunned silence. *Too late.*

She turned and walked back to her car, shoulders sagging, the check still clutched in her hand. The house she'd already imagined filled with warmth and laughter and second chances — gone.

She sat behind the wheel, staring through the windshield at the "Under Contract" sign as a light rain began to fall. Time was running out. And she was back to square one.

Intruder

Justine was in the shower when a loud crash jolted her. Her heart pounded as she shut off the water, grabbed a towel, and listened.

"Sara?" she called out.

"Get out of this house, James!" Sara's voice, panicked and sharp, echoed through the hallway.

Justine threw on jeans and a T-shirt, water still dripping from her hair, and sprinted down the hall. At Sara's door, she froze.

A towering man loomed over Sara, his hand raised. "I'll teach you to mess with me," he growled — and slapped her across the face.

Justine backed away, lungs tight with fear. She flung open the hall closet and grabbed Blake's baseball bat. He had once wanted to keep a gun in the house, but she had refused. Now she wished she hadn't.

When she returned, James was yanking at Sara's shirt. "Leave me alone!" Sara screamed, stumbling backward, blouse torn open, chest heaving.

"Get away from her!" Justine shouted, gripping the bat and lifting it over her shoulder. "Leave now, or I'll call the police!"

James turned, snarling. Justine swung the bat hard, aiming for the back of his head—but it landed on his shoulder. He stumbled, then charged, swatting her aside like she weighed nothing. She crashed to the floor, the bat skidding across the room, landing near Sara.

Justine scrambled to her knees. "Get out!" she yelled.

But James just laughed, blood staining his lip from her punch.

Then Sara moved.

She grabbed the bat, eyes blazing, and swung. The crack of wood against bone was sickening. James collapsed to his knees. He tried to rise, gripping the edge of the bed—but Sara struck again. And again. Until he stopped moving.

The room went still. Sara, covered in blood, let the bat fall from her trembling hands.

Justine crawled forward, checking his pulse. "He's dead," she whispered. "Oh my God, Sara. He's dead."

Sara crumpled to the floor, voice a choked whisper. "Are you sure?"

"Yes," Justine said. "We need to call the police."

"No! No—you can't." Sara clutched Justine's wrist. "They'll arrest me."

"It was self-defense. You were protecting yourself."

"Not with *my* record. No one will believe that. Please, Justine." Her eyes filled with desperate tears. "You know how the system works. You've seen it screw women like us."

Justine hesitated. Her stomach twisted.

"Nobody knows he's here," Sara said, voice low, urgent. "We can bury him. Out at Lover's Lane—no one will find him. Just say you never saw him. Please. If you ever cared about me, help me."

"I want to help, but I can't cover this up. That makes me an accessory."

Sara's voice turned icy. "It was *your* bat. If I go down, you go down. We both know the system doesn't give women second chances."

Justine's mind raced—images of prison bars, courtrooms, false accusations. Her pulse throbbed in her temples.

"Give me your car keys," Sara said. "I'll do it myself."

"You can't," Justine snapped. "His blood is all over you, all over the room."

"Peroxide. It'll lift the blood from the carpet." Her voice cracked. "Do you have any?"

Justine stared at her, shocked. "You've lost your mind."

"I'm begging you."

Justine looked at James's broken body. Her hands were shaking.

"No," she said finally, voice firm. "I'm calling the police. It's the right thing to do."

Sara didn't stop her this time. She just sat there, knees hugged to her chest, eyes hollow.

*****

The ambulance careened down the street, its siren slicing through the quiet of the neighborhood. Neighbors clustered outside, drawn by the flashing lights. The paramedics stepped out and pushed through the crowd toward Justine's front door.

At the same moment, Blake pulled into the driveway. He spotted the coroner's van and quickened his pace. The coroner, a colleague from other scenes, greeted him with a grim nod. They spoke in hushed tones near the curb.

Inside, the paramedics maneuvered the gurney down the narrow hallway.

"Do you have an old blanket, miss?" one asked. "It'll help us move him."

Justine numbly nodded, went to the linen closet, and retrieved an old quilt. She laid it out on the bedroom floor, avoiding James's shattered face. Her stomach turned. She gagged, barely keeping the bile down.

The paramedics rolled the body onto the blanket. Blood soaked through the fabric, leaving a gruesome trail as they lifted him into a body bag. The zipper's rasp echoed like a final punctuation mark.

As they wheeled the gurney out, onlookers strained to see.

"For Christ's sake—stand back!" one of the paramedics barked.

They pushed the gurney into the back of the ambulance and slammed the doors shut.

Justine stood at the edge of the crowd, holding a trembling Sara, who wept uncontrollably.

"I killed him," she sobbed. "I killed James."

Police officers separated them and led Sara to a patrol car to take her downtown for questioning.

Inside, crime scene tape stretched across the guest room doorway. Detectives snapped photos, marked blood spatter, and collected evidence. Blake and Justine sat silently on the porch, wrapped in blankets like survivors of a storm.

"You okay?" Blake asked gently.

Justine nodded, eyes glazed. "There's so much blood... I don't know if I can clean it."

"I'll take care of it," Blake said, wrapping an arm around her shoulders.

Hours passed. Finally, the lead detective stepped outside.

"You folks can go back in now," he said. Without another word, he and his partner slipped into their car and drove off into the night.

Blake rose and helped Justine to her feet. He peeled the crime scene tape from the doorway. Together, they stepped inside.

The room was in chaos. Blood had splattered across the bed, the walls, and the window. Justine looked down at her shirt. It was stained red. She rubbed at it absently, as if she could erase what had happened. A piece of tissue clung to the fabric — she couldn't tell if it was skin or brain matter.

"Go shower," Blake said. "I'll start in here. Try to get some rest."

"I don't think I can sleep."

"There are sedatives in the medicine cabinet. Take one, Justine. Please."

She nodded and retreated to the bedroom. The pill sat on the nightstand beside a glass of water. She stared at it for a long time. In the distance, she could hear the water running in the guest room as Blake scrubbed. Guilt pressed down on her like a weight.

She rose and returned.

Blake looked up, startled. "You didn't sleep?"

She shook her head. "I didn't take the sedative. This is my fault. I brought her here. I need to help."

Blake didn't argue. "Grab the Windex under the sink."

He pulled a bone fragment from the carpet and dropped it into a plastic bag. Justine returned with paper towels and glass cleaner. Together, they scrubbed until the blood was gone — or at least hidden.

When the work was done, Blake poured two shots of whiskey.

"Here," he said, handing her a glass. "It'll help us sleep."

They climbed into bed, drained and hollow. The room was dark, quiet — except for their breathing.

Justine curled against him, clinging as if she might disappear.

And for the rest of the night, they held each other, too exhausted to speak, too haunted to sleep.

Sara confessed to killing James but refused to elaborate.

"I killed him," she said flatly, her voice devoid of emotion. "That's all you need to know."

Blake leaned across the interrogation table, desperation tightening his features. "Sara, please. Give me something I can use in your defense. Maybe it was temporary insanity. Maybe you were provoked —"

"I wasn't insane," she cut in. "I'm glad he's dead."

He exhaled sharply, trying to keep his composure. "Do you even understand what that means? You could be facing life without parole. Or worse — lethal injection."

Sara stared blankly past him. "I don't care."

"You'll never see your children again."

"My in-laws made sure of that a long time ago. They've already poisoned my kids against me. James may be dead, but they'll always remember me as the monster he painted."

Whispers and headlines followed the pre-trial. Rumors swirled that Justine was complicit — it *had* happened in her home, after all — but Sara never wavered in her confession. "I did it alone," she insisted, even as Blake fought to keep her out of jail until the trial.

Justine testified on her behalf, and for a while, it looked like Sara might get a fair shot. But the judge wasn't convinced. He deemed her a flight risk and ordered her held.

Blake put up the bail himself, convincing the court to let Sara stay under house supervision. That night, the house was unusually still. Sara barely touched her dinner, muttered goodnight, and disappeared into the guest room.

*****

The next morning, Blake and Justine sat at the kitchen table, quietly sipping their coffee. Neither spoke much. Both watched the clock.

"She should be up by now," Justine said, glancing at the time again. "Her hearing is in an hour."

Blake nodded. "Maybe you should check on her."

Justine walked down the hall and knocked on the door. "Sara?" No answer. She knocked again, harder. "Sara, you'll be late for court. Open up."

Blake joined her. "Everything okay?"

"She's not answering. The door's locked."

"I'll grab a screwdriver."

Together, they removed the door from its hinges. The moment it swung open, Justine rushed to the bed.

Sara lay motionless. Her skin was pale and clammy, and her eyes rolled back. An empty pill bottle rested on the nightstand.

Justine's voice trembled. "Blake—call an ambulance!"

The same paramedics who had come weeks ago stormed back into the house, navigating familiar hallways. They lifted Sara onto the gurney with practiced urgency and disappeared into the siren-lit morning.

But it was too late.

Sara's heart had stopped en route to the hospital.

Justine sat on the porch long after the ambulance was gone, her arms wrapped around herself as if to hold together the pieces of a story still unraveling.

Was this her curse? To try and save broken women, only to lose them anyway?

Inside, Blake quietly closed the door to Sara's now-empty room. For a long time, neither of them spoke.

Grief settled over the house like a fog that refused to lift.

Birth Control

With Sara gone, Justine and Blake began the slow work of healing. Blake hired a new paralegal, offloaded a few clients to his partner, and even called in sick now and then just to spend time with her. They took long weekend drives upstate, aimlessly winding through backroads. Estate sales became their thing — Blake called it *pickin'*. He sifted through boxes of old records, tarnished jewelry, and forgotten keepsakes, always searching for treasure. To Justine, most of it was junk, but the quiet fun of doing it together made it worthwhile.

At home, life softened. They shared cartons of Chinese food on the couch. They made love. They ordered pizza. They made love again. They curled up to binge-watch old TV shows. Then made love once more. Justine did everything she could to make Blake smile again. But still, there was one thing she couldn't give him. Not yet.

A baby.

Blake wanted one. Desperately. And she couldn't put him off forever. But the idea left her breathless, unsure. Her doctor had warned her against taking the pill — too risky with her family's history of breast cancer and heart disease. Her mother's face flickered across her mind like a phantom. There one second, gone the next.

Justine spotted her running shoes by the door. She needed air. Needed clarity. Running always helped.

Outside, the July heat clung to her like a wet sheet. Even in shorts and a tank top, she felt overdressed. The pavement burned beneath her feet, but she pushed forward, the rhythm of her sneakers syncing with the churn of her thoughts.

A baby might fix this… pull us closer again.

But was that a reason to bring a child into the world?

The sky cracked open, and rain poured down. Heavy, cleansing, welcome. It soaked her skin and the scorched earth alike. By the time she got home, she was dripping but lighter somehow. She took off her sneakers and peeled off her socks.

The answering machine flashed.

Beep. "Hello, this is Mr. Pennington, the new warden at Lowell Correctional. A position has opened up for a youth counselor. If you're interested, please call at your earliest convenience."

Justine stared at the machine. Her heart kicked up. It was the kind of opportunity she hadn't dared to hope for. The young girls inside had always broken her heart — kids who'd made grown-up mistakes and were now paying grown-up prices. Some were barely old enough to drive. She knew their stories. Knew their pain.

That night, over dinner, she told Blake about the call.

She saw the flicker of disappointment in his eyes.

"Why would you go back there?" he asked quietly. "It took years to get you out."

Justine set down her fork. "Because I can't forget what I saw inside. There are so many women who never got a fair shot. Some of them are just kids. If I can be the person who makes a difference — even for one of them — I have to try."

Blake looked down at his plate, then back up. "I thought we were going to start our family."

"I want that too," she said, reaching for his hand. "But not yet. I need to do this first. These girls... they need someone. Once I know I've done my part, once I feel I've really helped, then we can start our family. I promise."

He gave a slow nod, though the sadness lingered in his expression. "I love you, Justine. I'll wait for you — as long as it takes."

Tears welled in her eyes, but she smiled through them. "Thank you, Blake. I love you, too."

*****

The next day, Justine returned the call to the warden.

"That's great news," he said when she accepted the position. "We'll just need you to sign a release of liability."

"When can I start?"

"As soon as next week, if you're ready. But we'll need a full medical exam and drug test results on file before you begin."

"I'll schedule an appointment with my doctor today."

"Perfect. Bring the paperwork with you on Monday. Report to the guard tower—your name will be on file, and they'll issue your clearance badge."

"I'll be there," she said, hanging up with a mix of excitement and nerves. Immediately, she dialed her doctor's office.

"We're completely booked," the receptionist said. "The earliest appointment I can offer is next month."

"Next month? That's too far off. I need a physical this week to start a new job."

"One moment," the receptionist said, placing her on hold.

Justine drummed her fingers on the counter as she sat through two elevator-music songs. Finally, the receptionist returned.

"If you can be here within twenty minutes, the doctor has a quick opening."

"I'm on my way!" Justine grabbed her purse and ran out the door.

At the office, they handed her a cup and directed her to the restroom for a urine sample, then led her to an exam room.

"The doctor will be in shortly," the nurse said. "Would you like a magazine?"

"No, thank you—but I'll take a bottle of water if you have one."

"Sure, I'll grab one from the nurse's station."

Before the water arrived, Dr. Kelly walked in.

"Hi, Justine. What brings you in today?"

"I'm starting a new job at the women's prison. They need a physical and a drug screening on file."

"We can do that. The blood results might take a couple of days depending on the lab's backlog, but since you were here recently, I'll do a basic physical and write up a report in the meantime."

"That's perfect. Thank you."

"What kind of work will you be doing?"

"Counseling the younger inmates."

Dr. Kelly raised her eyebrows with a smile. "That sounds like a great fit for you."

"I hope so. I'm a little nervous. Prison isn't exactly my favorite place, but I made a promise to myself—and to others—that I'd go back and help. A lot of these girls don't even know their rights. They need someone who's been there."

"That's right—you earned your law degree. Congratulations. I thought you were going into private practice?"

"I wanted to, but I can't practice until I take the Bar exam. Still working on that."

"Well, let me know if I can help in any way. At the very least, I'll vouch for your character. And if you ever need a referral, I'll make time to write one."

"Thank you, Dr. Kelly. That means a lot."

"As soon as I get a minute to breathe, I'll write something up for you."

Justine smiled. "I really appreciate it."

Later that evening, she returned home to an empty house. Blake was still at the office. Rather than head out for her usual run, she poured a glass of wine, grabbed a book, and curled up in the patio chair. The sun was setting behind the trees, and for the first time in a long while, the quiet didn't feel so heavy.

Young Prisoners

On the first day of her new job, Justine woke up with a pit in her stomach. Her nerves rattled like wind chimes in a storm. She brewed a cup of peppermint tea, hoping it would calm the queasiness. As she sipped, the phone rang. She rushed to answer, expecting Blake.

"Hello?"

"Mrs. Sullivan? This is the nurse from Dr. Kelly's office. We received your lab results this morning."

Justine straightened. "Is everything all right?"

"Well, you're... positive."

"Positive? Positive for what?"

The nurse chuckled. "You're pregnant, my dear. Congratulations."

Justine froze. "What? No, that can't be. That has to be a mistake."

"The test is 99.9 percent accurate," the nurse said gently.

"Shit," Justine whispered.

The realization hit her hard. She had been careless—no pills, no precautions—for the past two months. Her hand drifted to her flat stomach.

"We'd like you to come in for a sonogram, just to determine how far along you are. Can you make it this afternoon?"

"I'm starting a new job today," Justine said. "I can't miss it. I'm only off on Fridays."

"Then I'll schedule you for next Friday. Take care, and again—congratulations."

"Shit," Justine said again, louder this time.

She stood there for a long moment, one hand still resting on her belly. There was no bump, no sign of life yet—but now she knew. And suddenly, everything felt different.

Blake would be thrilled. He had wanted this. But she wasn't ready—not yet. She couldn't tell him. Not now. If he knew, he might insist she back out of her new position at the prison.

No, she'd wait until after the sonogram. One thing at a time.

She squared her shoulders, grabbed her keys, and headed out the door, pushing the thought aside—at least for today.

*****

From the moment Justine stepped through the gates of the prison, her body stiffened. The memories came flooding back—the fights, the screaming, the psychological warfare that played out day after day. Fiona was still there, as menacing as ever. Inmates gave her a wide berth, avoiding eye contact when she bullied some poor, defenseless newcomer. Even the guards steered clear, often forming quiet alliances with her just to keep the peace. As awful as she was, Fiona maintained a twisted sort of order.

Justine's arrival sent ripples through the hive. Fiona and her cronies huddled together, watching her with narrowed eyes, as if already plotting.

Mr. Pennington led her to a small office in the admin wing. It was as bleak as the rest of the prison — white walls, scuffed linoleum tiles, a desk, two chairs, and a computer. The flickering fluorescent light overhead cast an anemic glow.

"I'll have maintenance check that light," he said, following her gaze. "Today's schedule is light — you'll see two young women up for early parole: Jennifer and Anna. I didn't want to overwhelm you on your first day."

"Thanks. I appreciate that."

"You came highly recommended by Mr. Atwood. I'm sure you won't disappoint."

Once alone, Justine powered on the aging computer and found it connected to the internet. Shortcuts on the desktop linked to housing authorities, rehab centers, and job placement resources. She unpacked her bag, hung a calendar on the wall, and made a mental note to bring in posters — anything to soften the sterile environment. On her way to the vending machine, she bought two Cokes and placed one across the desk for her first client.

A young woman with long braids pinned over her head stepped inside.

"Hi, are you Justine?"

"I am. You must be Jennifer."

She giggled. "Guilty."

Her perfume couldn't mask the stale cigarette odor clinging to her clothes.

"Have a seat. Would you like a soda?"

"What I really want is a cigarette."

"Sorry. No smoking allowed."

Jennifer grinned. "Just wanted to see your reaction. But yeah, I'll take the Coke." She took a sip. "Ahh. That's the best thing I've tasted in months."

Justine smiled. "Glad you like it. Let's get started. Are you married?"

"No, but I had a boyfriend. We lived together for eight years. He ditched me for another woman while I was in here. Tossed all my stuff in a dumpster."

"Do you have family you can stay with when you're released?"

"They cut me off when I got with that meth-head. Haven't taken a call since."

"There's a halfway house. Strict rules — 90-day limit, job required, and only one meal a day. But it's a start."

"I've worked as a cashier. Maybe I can find something — if they'll hire an ex-con."

"There are employers on our list willing to give second chances. Maybe start as a stock clerk. Build trust."

"Stock clerks don't get paid shit. How am I supposed to afford rent?"

"I get it. We can get you on the list for low-income housing now. The wait is long, but the sooner you apply, the better."

"What happens if I don't find a place?"

"Then it's transitional housing. Not ideal — unsafe, high relapse rates. Best to avoid it."

"When do I get out?"

"In two weeks."

"Well then," Justine said, smiling. "We've got work to do."

Jennifer stood, then turned back. "Hey, why'd you ask about my hair?"

"I noticed you pinned up your braids."

Jennifer nodded. "It's getting rough in here. Long hair's the first thing they grab in a fight."

Justine nodded thoughtfully. "Thanks for the chat. And the insight."

After Jennifer left, Justine checked the clock. Twelve-thirty. She unwrapped the tuna sandwich she'd packed, but the smell made her queasy. She sipped her Coke instead and reviewed the halfway house regulations. The more she read, the more disheartened she became. Ninety days. One meal. No real support. And with limited housing options, many women were set up to fail — competing for the same few resources as those without a criminal record.

What they needed was a real place to transition — a place to heal and rebuild.

Justine opened a browser and searched "women's housing." Most were shelters for domestic abuse survivors. Others were job placement agencies. Nothing fit the vision she had in her head. A place for women like Jennifer. Like Anna. Like herself.

She imagined it again. A haven. A launchpad. *The House of Justice.*

Justine was pulled from her reverie when a soft voice said, "Hi, I'm Anna."

Justine looked up. A delicate woman with honey-blonde hair and sad brown eyes stood in the doorway, fingering a heart-shaped locket.

"Come in. I've been expecting you. Would you like a drink? I meant to grab another soda, but I lost track of time."

"That's okay."

Justine opened Anna's file. "You have a daughter, right? Abby?"

"She's six. I was three when I got locked up."

"Is she with her father?"

"No. He's doing thirty years. She's with my mother-in-law."

"Do you have a lawyer?"

"A court-appointed one. At least she's a woman. Maybe she'll understand. Men don't usually care about separating a kid from her mom."

"Where will you stay after release?"

"My cousin owns a flower shop. She said I can crash in her spare room and help with the business. I just want my daughter back before my mother-in-law poisons her against me."

"I know a bit about family court," Justine said. "But not enough to advise you properly. Let me do some research and get back to you."

Anna wiped a tear. "Thank you. That gives me hope. I don't let myself hope much—it usually turns into heartbreak."

When Anna left, Justine dug into custody law. She discovered that unless a parent is proven unfit, courts favor reunification. A grandparent couldn't just take custody based on money or status.

Then I'll make sure Anna is ready, she thought.

With five minutes left in her shift, she packed her bag. Tomorrow would come fast—and there was work to do.

Abducted

With her car keys in hand, Justine passed Fiona in the hall, standing outside the laundry room. Two women came out and handed something to her. Fiona tucked it into the elastic waistband of her pants. Justine recognized them as Wilma and Becky — two of Fiona's partners in crime.

Justine flinched as the fire alarms blared. Guards rushed down the hallway. Panicked women ran toward the exits as black smoke poured from the laundry room. She turned to leave, but Fiona and her crew blocked her path. Justine's throat constricted. Fiona stepped behind her while Wilma and Becky moved into position in front. She was surrounded.

The women moved like a unit. Justine scanned her surroundings, searching for a way out. Her eyes darted as she fumbled for the valet key hidden in her fob. Clutching it between her knuckles like a weapon, she briefly considered slashing Fiona's throat.

Fiona kicked the back of her calf. "Don't look to the guards to save your ass."

Justine collapsed to the ground, dropping her keys. Wilma and Becky closed in, taking turns punching her in the ribs. She looked up at Fiona, silently begging her to make them stop. Her bottom lip quivered, her eyes welled with tears, and her stomach churned with an unnatural flutter.

The baby. They're going to kill my baby.

"Please, don't," she sobbed.

Becky let out a jagged laugh that sounded like broken glass. She was about to kick Justine again, but Fiona stopped her.

"Save some for later. Grab her purse and make sure the phone is off. Then toss it in the trash."

Fiona pointed a pistol at Justine's head. "Get on your feet."

Justine struggled to stand, but her battered knees kept giving out. A blinding pain shot from her wrist to her shoulder. Fiona twisted her arm again and shoved her toward the cafeteria.

"No. I'm not going with you," Justine said.

"Let's just kill her here," Wilma suggested.

"There's a fire," Justine pleaded. "We need to get out."

"That wasn't a fire, lady. Just a distraction." Fiona pressed the gun harder into Justine's head.

"Where did you get that gun?"

"I have my ways. Now shut up before you eat a bullet."

"What do you want? Why are you doing this?"

"You're the prison commissioner's darling," Becky said. "Very valuable to us. I'm sure the Board of Prisons will meet all our demands for your release."

"There's no way you'll get away with this," Justine said. "You can't just walk out of prison."

"Oh, don't worry about that. Becky made nice with a guard. He's our ride out of here."

"They'll shoot you before you make it out. Let me help you. I can talk to the warden."

Fiona aimed the gun at her again. "You think you're some kind of saint, Justine? You're just as flawed as the rest of us. The only difference is you had more chances."

"So you're blaming me for your choices?"

"It's people like you that keep us down."

"All I've ever wanted was to help women."

"Oh, please. You don't give a shit about us. You think you're high and mighty just because you know the law. I bet that lawyer husband of yours is starting to see through you."

"Don't talk about my husband!" Justine snapped, her composure slipping.

Fiona's jaw clenched. She released the safety and slid her finger onto the trigger.

"Do it, you piece of shit," Justine whispered, eyes shut, resigned to her fate.

Click.

Justine opened her eyes and drew in a breath of sweet relief.

"What's wrong with this thing?" Fiona yelled.

"I don't know," Wilma said. "It was in the laundry bin. Maybe it caught some lint."

"You idiot!" Fiona screamed. "I told you to tell Mur to wrap it in plastic." She shoved the gun back in her waistband.

"You're getting awfully bossy, Fiona," Wilma said. "I'm getting sick of it."

"Jesus." Fiona's eyes blazed. She balled her fists and took a fighting stance, but Wilma tackled her. They rolled on the floor, fists flying.

"I'll punch your fucking eyes to the back of your skull," Wilma growled, her jaw clenched so tight Justine could see the bones.

"Stop it!" Becky screamed. She pulled a switchblade from her boot and flicked it open. "Fiona's my friend!" she shouted, slashing Wilma's face. A ribbon of blood dripped down Wilma's cheek.

Wilma lunged for the knife, but Becky jammed the four-inch blade into her stomach. Wilma wailed, eyes blinking rapidly. She rolled onto her side, coughing and wheezing, blood pooling beneath her.

A guard burst through the side door. "Help!" Justine cried—but he didn't react. No sympathy. No recognition.

It was Allen Murphy.

"Took you long enough, Mur," Fiona said. "Is the van ready?"

"Fuck," he muttered when he saw Wilma. The vein in his forehead bulged as he knelt to check her pulse. "She's still alive."

"Let's go," Fiona barked.

"What about Wilma?" Becky asked. "We can't leave her."

Fiona snapped her fingers in Wilma's face. "Get up, Wilma." She yanked the knife out and wiped the blade on her pants. Wilma opened her eyes, and Fiona dragged her to her feet.

"Get her to the van," she ordered Becky, then turned to Justine. "Her, too."

"No!" Justine cried.

"You're coming with us. You're our shield."

"Please. If you kill me, you'll have my blood on your hands."

Fiona laughed. "You think I give a shit about your blood?"

Justine tried to stand, but her knees kept locking. Fiona dragged her to the side door.

"If you don't use those damn legs, I'll break 'em."

"Hurry before they realize you're gone," Allen said. He jumped in the driver's seat. Becky sat in the back, cradling Wilma.

"Damn it," Fiona said. "My gun jammed again."

"You're not getting mine," Allen snapped.

"Release the clip," Becky suggested. "Maybe something's blocking it."

Fiona ejected the shell, blew out the dust, and reloaded. "There. That should do it."

She shoved Justine in the front seat and climbed into the back. Pointing the gun, she warned, "Try anything, and I'll blow your head off."

Allen drove toward the gates. Recognizing him, the guard waved them through the first checkpoint.

Justine widened her eyes, silently pleading for help—but the tower guard didn't notice.

As the van approached the second gate, alarms blared, and a voice rang out over the speakers:

"THIS IS A LOCKDOWN. NO ONE IS TO ENTER OR EXIT UNTIL FURTHER NOTICE."

"Sorry, Allen. You'll have to turn around," the control officer said.

"Floor it!" Fiona screamed.

The van crashed through the gate.

"Take the next right. There's an old bridge over the river."

"I know a back road," Becky said. "It's shut down—no traffic."

The van bounced along a rough dirt road. They could see the bridge ahead, but a police cruiser spotted them and gave chase, lights flashing, sirens wailing. Gravel sprayed behind the tires as the van accelerated.

"Step on it!" Fiona yelled. "They're gaining on us!"

Fiona rolled down her window and fired at the cruiser, blowing out the passenger-side tire. The patrol car flipped, skidding on its side, smoke pouring from the hood.

"We did it!" Becky cried. "But Wilma needs a doctor—she's fading fast!"

"Stop whining," Fiona said coldly. She turned to Wilma and shot her in the chest. Wilma's eyes widened. With one last surge of adrenaline, she sat up—then collapsed in a pool of blood.

"Yep. Works just fine now." Fiona slid open the van door and shoved Wilma's body out.

Becky sat dazed. "You're not going to shoot me, too, are you?"

"Don't be a twit. You're my best friend."

Allen looked in the side mirror and saw Wilma hit the curb.

"What the fuck, Fiona? Why the hell did you do that?"

"She was dead weight."

On the Run

The vibrations of the road rattled through Justine's body. Her jaw clenched against the pain — then *crack*. A sharp splinter of tooth landed on her tongue. She tasted blood and panic. Her heart pounded so violently that it made her dizzy. Unable to hold it together, she screamed.

"*Shut up!*" Fiona snarled, smacking the side of her head with the butt of the pistol. Justine's stomach clenched. Her mouth went dry. Blood trickled from her lip and down her chin. She fell silent.

In the driver's seat, Allen shifted uncomfortably. "So... where's the money you promised me?"

Fiona smirked. "That's the million-dollar question everyone wants to know. Just get on the highway and head north."

Allen glanced at her through the rearview mirror. "How do you know it's still there?"

"Don't worry. It's there. We buried it after the robbery. Me and Derik. Then he croaked."

"Did you kill him?" Allen asked.

"No. I loved Derik." Her voice softened for a beat. "He was the only guy who ever laughed at my jokes."

"Then how'd he die?"

"He took a bullet to the gut at the bank. Bled all over my car, but he was a trooper. Held out until we made it to an old, abandoned barn."

"That's where the money is?"

"Yeah. We buried it."

The van sped north on I-95 for six long, silent hours.

"I'm hungry," Becky finally said. "Can we stop for food?"

"I need gas anyway," Allen muttered.

"Next gas station with a food mart," Fiona ordered. She leaned forward and pressed the pistol against Justine's temple. "Try to signal anyone, and I swear I'll blow your head clean off."

A Circle-K appeared off the exit. Allen pulled in and stopped at the pump.

"Becky," Fiona said, "go inside and pinch us some food."

"Why me? You come with."

"Who's gonna watch the hostage?" Fiona raised an eyebrow.

"Shit," Becky muttered. She slung a large shoulder bag over her arm, opened the side door, and climbed out.

*****

Twenty minutes later, they were back on the highway.

"Hurry—it's getting dark," Allen said. "How much longer?"

"Just a few more miles."

"Are you sure you know where you're going?"

"Of course I do," Fiona snapped, but doubt flickered in her eyes. She scanned the landscape. "Just keep driving. The exit should be coming up soon."

A few minutes later, she shouted, "That's it! Get off and turn west."

After another forty minutes, Allen's patience cracked. "I don't think you remember where this place is."

Anguish swept across Fiona's face. "Shit. This is farm country. All the barns look the same."

"I don't think we're going to find it tonight," Allen said. "Maybe we should pull over and wait until morning."

Fiona's eyes widened. "There." She pointed to a narrow dirt road. "Take that one."

Allen turned. At the end of the road sat a weathered barn with a sagging tin roof, on the verge of collapse. He cut the engine. They climbed out and went inside. The air was stagnant. No windows. No light.

Derik still lay in the corner—a skeleton of a man, long picked over by animals.

Fiona grabbed some shovels. "Come on, let's get that money."

They walked to a clearing behind the barn, where a narrow path led to an open field.

"I think this is the spot," Fiona said, handing Justine a shovel. "Dig."

Justine looked down. "I can't see — it's too dark."

"She's right," Allen added. "We'll have to wait until morning."

"I guess you're right," Fiona said, her stomach growling. "I'm hungry anyway."

"Where are we sleeping?" Becky asked.

"In the barn."

"With the dead body?"

Fiona laughed. "You're not afraid of ghosts, are you, Becky?"

Back inside, Fiona rummaged through Becky's shoulder bag. "What did you get us to eat?"

Becky emptied it: crackers, a bag of chips, two bottles of water, and some beef jerky.

"What the hell is this?"

"It's all I could get. Some nosy clerk was eyeballing me." She handed out the jerky. "It's meat!"

"No, thank you," Justine said. "I'm not hungry — but I do have to use the bathroom."

"There's a bucket by the door."

"But..."

Becky snickered. "We won't look."

Justine, grateful she wore a skirt, turned away and squatted over the bucket. Humiliated but relieved, she stood and looked out the barn doors.

"One more thing," Fiona said, approaching her. "Just in case you get any ideas."

She kicked Justine hard in the shin with her prison-grade boot. Justine crumpled to the ground.

"There's no reason for that," Allen muttered. "The main road is miles back. She couldn't walk it if she tried. Let's just get some sleep so we can dig up that money and get out of here."

"Please, God," Justine whispered, looking up at the stars. *If You exist, help me.* She limped to a corner of the barn and curled into a fetal position. She woke to the smell of rot and dampness seeping into her clothes. Her blouse was caked with dirt and sweat. Morning air clung to the barn, but the heat would rise quickly.

Fiona, Becky, and Allen nibbled leftover crackers and jerky.

"You want breakfast?" Allen asked.

Justine's stomach turned, but she needed the strength. "I'll take some crackers."

As she ate, her captors argued about where to go once they had the money. Fiona wanted to flee to the North Georgia mountains. Allen argued for the Appalachian Trail in Virginia.

"I've always wanted to see the Blue Ridge Mountains," Becky chimed in.

Outnumbered, Fiona scowled. "Fine. Let's dig."

Justine's bruised leg ached. After three shovelfuls of dirt, she collapsed. "I can't do it," she cried.

"Oh, stop being such a baby." Fiona grabbed the shovel. "Let's get this done."

Moments later, they hit something solid — a leather satchel. Allen pried it from the ground and opened it. Neatly stacked bills spilled out.

"Just like I said," Fiona grinned, snatching the bag. "You'll get your cut later. Let's go."

Justine's legs throbbed, but she forced herself into the van.

Back on I-95, Fiona and Becky eagerly counted the cash.

Justine leaned toward Allen and whispered, "Why are you doing this?"

Allen's jaw clenched. He glanced at Fiona, then whispered, "I'm sorry. Try not to speak. This'll all be over soon."

His eyes suddenly widened as they rounded a bend.

Curious, Justine pulled herself up.

Four patrol cars blocked the road.

"Roadblock!" Fiona shouted. "Turn around — cut through that open field!"

Allen slowed the van.

"Allen!" Fiona barked. "Why are you stopping?"

"You're going back to prison, lady. That's your ride."

Fiona's eyes went wild. "You bastard! You set me up!"

She raised the gun and pulled the trigger. *Click.* Nothing.

The gun jammed.

Allen reached for the strap around his ankle — but Fiona was faster. She grabbed the same knife she'd pulled from Wilma's gut.

Allen slammed the brakes and killed the engine. "You don't want to do this, Fiona."

"I'm already in for first-degree murder. What's one more body?"

She reached around the seat and slashed his throat. Blood gushed down his shirt as he gurgled and slumped onto the horn.

"Get out of the van!" a deputy barked, gun drawn. "On your knees — hands on your head!"

Fiona and Becky bolted, but Justine dropped to her knees, hands behind her head.

Two gunshots rang out.

She opened her eyes.

Becky lay bleeding past the van, a bullet in her leg.

Fiona was farther down the road, face down in a pool of blood — dead.

An officer yanked open the driver's door and caught Allen before his body hit the pavement.

"Damn it, Allen," he whispered. "Why didn't you jump out and run? A dead hero's no good to anyone."

Justice

Justine felt relieved to be home. She tossed her clothes into a pile on the floor and stepped into the shower. The water was too hot, but she stood under the spray, letting it dig into her muscles. Soil had embedded itself beneath her fingernails, and she scrubbed until her fingertips throbbed. Reaching for the shampoo, she massaged it into her scalp. A sharp pain shot through her finger — something had pierced the skin. A thin stream of blood spiraled down the drain, followed by tiny shards of glass from the shattered windshield.

She flipped her hair forward, letting the water flush out the glass and the bloody shampoo. Then she paused. A flutter stirred in her belly — and she smiled.

After drying off, she pulled on a pair of sweatpants and a long-sleeve shirt. Opening the window, she let the crisp morning air kiss her face. She exhaled the breath she hadn't realized she'd been holding, and the tension began to melt from her body.

Downstairs, Blake stood in the kitchen making coffee. She hadn't told him about the baby — not yet.

"How are you feeling?" he asked when she walked in.

"I'm fine." She looked him in the eye. "And so is our baby."

His brow furrowed. "Baby?"

"Yes." She took a breath. "I found out I was pregnant right before I took the job. I was going to tell you, but... I didn't think you'd let me work at the prison. I planned to tell you when I got home. I just... never got the chance."

He rushed to her, wrapping her in his arms, then pressed his hand gently to her stomach. "The baby — is it okay?"

"Calm down." She laughed. "The baby's fine. I felt him kicking in the shower."

"Him?"

"Maybe. It was a strong kick."

Blake chuckled. "If it's a girl, she's probably tough as nails — like her mom. You and that baby have been through hell."

Justine's voice softened. "It was all I could think about while I was being held hostage. If anything had happened to me, you never would've known I was carrying the beginnings of a new life."

He kissed her forehead. "We need to get you to the doctor. I don't want to take any chances."

"I agree — but I need something to eat first. We're starving."

"I'll make you pancakes," he said, already heading for the pantry.

As she sat at the table, the warmth of home wrapped around her. But her thoughts drifted to the prison—the women she'd left behind.

"I want to stay in touch with the women," she said. "But I know you don't want me to go back."

Blake turned from the stove. "I don't. I know how much they mean to you, but after what happened…"

"I can't just turn my back on them. Jennifer needs a job. Anna still doesn't have custody of her daughter. I made them promises."

He set the pancake batter aside and walked over. "I get it. But your guilt won't help them—it could hurt you. We can support them in other ways. I can represent Anna in court, and you can help Jennifer find a job."

Justine nodded slowly. "That's true… but there are so many women in prison who need legal counsel. I want to help them, too."

"Then maybe you can counsel them from home," he offered. "Virtual consultations. Letters. Phone calls."

"Maybe," she said, considering. "I'll talk to the warden."

*****

While Justine was at the doctor's office, Blake called her father. He was waiting at their house when they returned home. Justine dropped her bag and fell into his arms.

"Justine," he said, pulling her close. "I've been worried sick. How's the baby?"

"He's fine. We saw him on the ultrasound."

"A boy!"

"Yes," she said, exchanging a look with Blake. "We've already chosen a name."

"What will we call the little man?"

"Ben. We're naming him after you."

Her father's face softened. "I'm honored."

He glanced at her belly and added, "I guess this means you won't be going back to work?"

"Not until the baby is born. Michael and Zoeie are taking over at the Justice House for now."

"Oh—that reminds me. You've got some mail waiting back at my house."

"I'll swing by and pick it up soon."

"There was something from the Bar Association. Maybe it's good news."

Later, Justine called Mr. Pennington, who informed her that both Jennifer and Anna had been released. He gave her their contact information.

She called Jennifer first.

"Hi, Justine." Jennifer let out a long breath.

Justine recognized the sound instantly. She could picture her lighting a cigarette, dragging it down to the nub, then stamping it out—but not completely.

"You're still smoking."

"Sorry," Jennifer replied. "It's the only pleasure I've got left."

"I heard what happened to you at the prison," Jennifer added. "That sucks."

"Tell me about it. I was lucky. Blake doesn't want me to take any more risks. What about you? Did you find a job yet?"

"No. I've filled out over a dozen applications. Not one callback."

"I have a friend at the power company. They're looking for a cleaner. Good pay. I can give you the number."

"That sounds great. I'll call today. Better yet, maybe I'll go in person."

"I'll write you a recommendation. That should help."

"Thank you, Justine. You're a good egg."

Justine laughed. *A good egg?* She hadn't heard that one in a while. She hung up and dialed Anna next, asking if she wanted to meet for lunch.

They met at a small café. Justine arrived first and waited at an outdoor table. A few minutes later, she saw Anna approaching in a bright yellow sundress and white sandals.

"You look like spring," Justine said, rising to hug her.

Anna did a little twirl. "You like? I got this number at the Salvation Army. Calvin Klein. You'd be surprised what you can find if you dig through the crap."

"It's fabulous. I'll go with you next time. My clothes are getting kind of tight."

Anna's eyes widened. "You're pregnant?"

Justine nodded, beaming. "It's a boy. We're naming him Ben, after my father."

Anna grinned. "Benny and the Jets!"

They both laughed, the weight of their pasts lifting briefly in the sun-drenched moment.

*****

On her way home, Justine stopped at the county administration offices to see Laura Mosely. They'd become good friends, and the receptionist was used to Justine's visits. She waved her straight through to the commissioner's office.

"Justine!" Laura cried, rising from her chair. "I've been so worried. Are you all right?"

"I'm a little bruised, but I'll be fine." Justine gave a small smile and rested a hand on her belly.

Laura's eyes narrowed. "Wait a minute—Justine, are you pregnant?"

"Yes," she said, a hint of amusement in her voice. "Blake finally got the job done. It's just what he wanted."

"And what about you?"

"I'm surprisingly happy," she said softly. "I'm actually looking forward to being a mother."

"I guess that means you won't be going back to work?"

"I wasn't planning to, but—"

"But what?"

Justine's eyes lit up. "The American Bar Association approved my application to take the Bar!"

Laura rushed over and hugged her. "Oh, I'm so happy for you, Justine!"

"Once I pass, I'll be able to hang my own shingle — and finally help those women trapped in the system."

"You will make a huge difference in their lives. I know it."

Justine sighed. "It's just too bad I can't buy the halfway house. They're going to tear it down next week."

"I wish we could save it too," Laura said. "But the state just doesn't have that kind of money in the budget."

"People need to know what's happening. These women shouldn't be invisible."

Laura nodded. "Then tell them. Go public. Alert the media. You'd be surprised — people donate to causes they care about."

Justine frowned. "I hate asking for money. So far, I've gotten a lot of flak from people who think I'm promoting government handouts. Why would they want to help?"

"Because not everyone thinks like that," Laura said. "Some people want to help. You just have to find them. It's worth a shot."

Justine hesitated. Public speaking had always terrified her. Even as a child, she could barely read in front of the class. Fear of making a mistake twisted her tongue, and sometimes she'd stutter, trying to force the words out while her mind raced ahead. She could already feel the old anxiety rising in her chest.

What if I say the wrong thing? What if people turn against me?

But now, she had something to fight for — the women still trapped inside — and the baby growing inside her.

Thanks to Commissioner Mosely, Justine already had the ear of several state lawmakers. She had two weeks to come up with a plan.

And this time, she wouldn't let fear stop her.

*****

"Justine, hurry up!" Blake nearly exploded with excitement. "You're on the evening news!"

Justine rushed into the living room. On the television screen, she saw herself standing beside a news reporter holding a microphone.

"I'm here today with Justine Morgan," the reporter announced. "She has found the courage to speak up for women struggling to get back on their feet after incarceration. Justine is raising funds to purchase a halfway house scheduled to close this month."

The camera cut to Justine, her expression steady, voice clear.

"These women are complex," she said. "They're not violent criminals. Most have been convicted of property crimes — larceny, theft, fraud — or drug offenses. Yes, they've made poor decisions, but many are capable of learning from their mistakes."

"I'm sure there are men in similar situations," the reporter said.

"Of course," Justine replied, "but women face unique challenges. Even though they work the same jobs and hours as men, they're more likely to live in poverty. Why? Because they're paid less. That wage gap keeps women dependent. And most of the time, they're also the sole custodians of their children. When a mother is incarcerated, the entire family suffers. So, we have to ask—why are so many women ending up in prison? Are they committing crimes just for the thrill of it? Or are these crimes tied to survival?"

"Are you saying the community should provide them with free housing?"

"No. I'm suggesting temporary support—just long enough for them to get an education or training. That should be the only requirement. Once they have skills, they can support themselves and their children. They just need a safety net while they rebuild their lives."

The reporter turned back to the camera. "There you have it. Justine Morgan isn't advocating for handouts—she's advocating for hope. For tools that help women thrive. American women are struggling to provide for themselves and their families. It's time we pull together as a community to help change that."

*****

Messages poured in from all over the state—small donations from people who believed in Justine's mission. Some sent a dollar, others five, ten, or twenty.

A few generous souls sent a hundred, which made Justine smile. One person even sent a check for a thousand dollars, and that made her cry.

"There are a lot of generous people in this town," she whispered, overwhelmed with gratitude.

The funds kept coming. In the end, they surpassed the amount needed to secure the mortgage. Justine used the extra money for renovations and long-overdue maintenance. The house was old. The wood floors were sun-faded and cracked, and the blinds — tucked away in a hall closet — were brittle and yellowed, with most of the slats missing.

Justine had a vision for the house — one of structure, dignity, and opportunity. She modeled it after a college dormitory. Each woman had her own room, and those with young children were given adjoining spaces. The rooms weren't meant for luxury, but for peace of mind and restful sleep. For entertainment, Justine converted an old room into a small auditorium with a large screen for movie nights. A business center was equipped with computers and a small library to promote reading and independent study.

Meals were taken together in the communal dining room, and each morning began with scheduled classes. Comfort wasn't the end goal — empowerment was. Justine believed that if a woman had the tools to build a better life, she wouldn't fall back on excuses. A daycare center was created for residents with children, staffed by the women themselves for a small wage, fostering both responsibility and community.

Thanks to scholarships and grant funding, every woman at Justice House had the opportunity to pursue an education or learn a trade.

Boxes of supplies began arriving — bedding, clothing, books, toys. Volunteers from the community came to help scrub, paint, and prepare the space. Together, they buffed the floors, hung curtains, and breathed new life into the house.

The ribbon-cutting ceremony was packed. County officials, prison administrators, Blake's law colleagues, the media, and many others from the community came to celebrate.

Her nameplate was hung, and the new sign went up.

"Justice House. A home for healing. A place to begin again."

Blake hugged her tightly. "I'm so proud of you," he whispered.

Laura raised her arms with a triumphant smile. "Now *that's* justice!"

Thank you for reading Justice Rules. Please post a review on Amazon.com and check out other books by Janet Sierzant.

Gemini Joe
Brooklyn Love Story
Sauce on Sunday
The Green Room
Asunder
A Made Man

Resources for Women

Homeless Women Reintegration Programs - Contact local reintegration programs specifically tailored for women coming out of prison. These programs often provide housing assistance, job training, counseling, and other supportive services to help with the transition into stable housing and employment.

Salvation Army - The Salvation Army may offer shelter and support services for homeless individuals, including women. They might provide temporary housing, meals, clothing assistance, and case management to help individuals secure stable housing and employment.

Grace Market Place - Grace Market Place is a local organization that offers various services to homeless individuals, including showers, meals, clothing, and access to resources for finding housing and employment.

United Against Poverty - United Against Poverty provides various services to individuals and families in need, including a crisis stabilization program, access to a food pantry, educational programs, and resources for finding stable housing and employment.

Homeless Assistance Resource Team (HART) - HART is a collaborative effort among local organizations and agencies to address homelessness in Indian River

County. They offer various services and resources to homeless individuals and families, including assistance with finding housing, accessing healthcare, and obtaining necessary identification documents.

County Jail Reentry Programs - Contact the County Jail to inquire about any reentry programs or resources available to individuals upon release from prison. They may provide referrals to local organizations or agencies that offer support to recently released individuals.

Women's Refuge Organizations - While primarily focused on assisting women facing domestic violence, Women's Refuge may offer resources and support to homeless women in need of assistance, including temporary shelter, counseling, and referrals to community resources.

211 Helpline - Dialing 2-1-1 can connect individuals with a variety of resources and services in their area, including emergency shelter, food assistance, healthcare, and support for reentry into the community after incarceration.

Job Placement Programs - Explore local job placement programs or workforce development initiatives that assist individuals with finding employment opportunities. These programs may offer job training, resume assistance, and connections to local employers willing to hire individuals with criminal backgrounds.

Faith-Based Organizations - Many churches and religious organizations in the Vero Beach area provide support and assistance to individuals in need, including homeless women reentering society after incarceration. Contact local churches or religious institutions to inquire about available resources and support services.